The Sacred Key

Natasha Dawn

Guardian Publishing

Copyright © 2015 Natasha Dawn

All rights reserved.

ISBN-13: 978-0-9940711-2-5

DEDICATION

To all the parents who would go to hell and back for their child...being a parent will forever be our greatest adventure.

CONTENTS

Prologue	1
Chapter One	9
Chapter Two	19
Chapter Three	24
Chapter Four	34
Chapter Five	38
Chapter Six	49
Chapter Seven	57
Chapter Eight	62
Chapter Nine	70
Chapter Ten	84
Chapter Eleven	92
Chapter Twelve	103
Chapter Thirteen	112
Chapter Fourteen	124
Chapter Fifteen - Azazel's Descent	136
Chapter Sixteen	144
Chapter Seventeen	150

Natasha Dawn

Chapter Eighteen - Blair's Escape	159
Chapter Nineteen	177
Chapter Twenty - Blair's Rescue	188
Chapter Twenty One	194
Chapter Twenty Two	206
Chapter Twenty Three	223
Chapter Twenty Four	235
Chapter Twenty Five	248
Chapter Twenty Six	262
Chapter Twenty Seven	275

ACKNOWLEDGMENTS

There are no words that can truly express the gratitude I have for my wonderful friend, and publisher, Candace. You pushed me and encouraged me to get my ideas down on paper and look what happened! To my Mom for just being you! Your love and support in everything I do has given me the strength and independence to take chances and find the next challenge in my life without fear. To my love Jon, and our three beautiful monkeys...even on the craziest of days, my love and pride for you all is limitless. Lastly, thank you to all my fellow book nerds; without us there would be no movies in Hollywood ;)

PROLOGUE

Run.

I hoofed it like hell hounds snapped at my ankles through the tall grass, pressing the tiny bundle tightly against my chest.

Blair.

The two words swirled in my head, my only thoughts. I couldn't have imagined the pure evil, the betrayal, the disregard for such a precious package. I ran like the wind, tapping into an unnatural strength, and still, I heard them closing in, coming for me. Coming for *him*.

The flashes of yellow and blue behind me lit

the way through thick trees, but they represented the imminent threat. I clenched my teeth against the voice in my head that didn't belong to me. *You're a coward. Cowards run. Men fight!* It blended into the background with the rest of the words pounding in my head, a cacophony of evil manipulation. *Stop! Turn back! He's safe with us!*

I gritted my teeth, growling in a whisper, "Just shut the hell up!"

My care package remained silent, as if sensing the danger of crying, and I patted his back, stumbled and recovered. I smelled the lake as I closed in, and the temperature cooled slightly, raising bumps on my skin as the heat of overexertion contrasted with the moist air. If Seth held to his word, he would be waiting in the Hummer, and I broke through the fog gathered in the basin around the water with a smile, the shiny black vehicle chromed out and glowing almost as brightly as my little brother's excitement.

He heard my heavy footsteps crunching the tall grass and poked his head out, waving his arm as if it would make me go faster. "Boy, am I glad to see you! Those fucking bitches aren't going to give up, are they?"

"Nope," I answered, climbing into the back seat, too out of breath and in too much of a hurry to go around. "And they aren't far behind. I don't even want to know what the hell they're shooting at me." I wrapped my jacket around Blair, supplementing the blankets to help block the chill in the air. I gazed at his tiny face and looked into the mismatched eyes, one emerald green and the other ocean blue, and I swallowed at the evidence proving he was exactly what the maniacal women had been waiting for. "We're safe now," I whispered, kissing him on the forehead. He just kept staring at me and, for a split second, I swear he smiled. Could newborns do that?

"Yeah, bro, it's like the Fourth of July out here. I thought they might have fried your ass! Maybe if you lost a little of that bulky muscle, you'd run faster." He chuckled and floored the gas. I reached for the seat belt, needing to protect myself and my son against Seth's penchant for driving like a bat out of hell.

Then I heard her, above the rest of the voices. I turned to look behind us, and there she stood, in her white silk nightgown at the tree line, as if she'd never given birth. *Damn, she was sexy.* I might have reconsidered my flight, if she wasn't such an evil witch. Literally. Instead, I wondered if Seth had brought his big fucking gun and where the hell it might be.

"Jax, my love...why are you leaving me? We're family. That's our child. Please come back," she said in that freaky mind speech. All this telepathic shit was going to give me a migraine. Staring back, I opened my mind for her to hear want I knew. As she absorbed the information, her eyes grew wide and crazed, her face red with a demonic expression.

"No!! I will find you! You cannot hide from the coven, Jax! You can't run from me!"

I shot her the middle finger. "Consider this a divorce." She disappeared into the mist as

Seth drove into the darkest night of the year.

My mind drifted as we drove, and I thought back to the day I learned I would be a father.

I leaned back on the couch, flipping channels, and Amelia sat by the fireplace, staring into the flames. "Jax, I'm pregnant."

The words blasted through my bored haze like a sledgehammer, and I sat up straight, turning to stare at her. "Are you fucking kidding me?" It probably wasn't the best response, but to my credit, I'd been zoned out, looking for a football game when she laid the news on me. That sort of mental whiplash can make the most decent of men say stupid shit.

She turned her icy blue stare on me, the reflection of the flames dancing around her irises. "What kind of a response is that? We *are* married. Don't you think it was bound to happen?"

I searched for words and stuttered, "Of course, but I thought we were going to take our time. I mean, we're still young and just starting out." I tried to speak calmly, but my heart beat so loud the sound drowned out my thoughts. She'd never looked at me with such disgust, and though I was admittedly in shock, the glare was too harsh for me to have imagined it.

She turned away, staring back at the fire and not speaking for several long minutes. "There is no time. I had no choice." She spoke so quietly I would have missed it if I wasn't watching her.

I shook my head, trying to clear my confusion. "What do you mean, you had no choice? We agreed to wait, and I didn't pressure you." My emotions were spinning out of control, and I breathed in through my nose, out through my mouth to regain my senses. How could she say that? I had given her nothing but love and respect. Where the fuck did she get off making it sound like I gave her an ultimatum?

And then, I realized, maybe the pressure came from someone else. My jaw muscle twitched. "It's those 'guides' you hang out with, isn't it?" God, I hated those bitches, and considering the way those meddling women looked at me every time they came over for their little meetings, like some messed up support group, the feeling was mutual.

She stood to leave, obviously irate, but I wasn't finished and grabbed her arm. "Wait, Amelia."

"Don't touch me!" she spat, flinging her hand out. Suddenly, I was airborne, flying backward through the air, into the kitchen, and scraping every counter and obstacle on the way by. I slammed into the wall, the wind knocked out of me, and I slid to the floor, dazed. What the hell? My wife weighed maybe 110 pounds soaking wet, and I'd been an offensive lineman in high school. Was it even possible she'd just tossed me across the house like a ragdoll?

I realized I lay on broken glass and had a chair leg digging into my spine, and Amelia approached me, her face an unfamiliar mask of hatred. She knelt beside me and placed her hand on my cheek. Her eyes were blue fire and carried a wicked gleam, and I heard her voice, though her mouth didn't move.

"I guess it's time. I'll have to teach you what kind of world you live in…my fallen angel."

Something surged through me, starting where she touched, and I passed out.

Amelia had never been family. She'd been a liar, a master at betrayal, manipulation, and fallacies. And Blair was *my* boy. I wouldn't let any harm come to him. Ever.

CHAPTER ONE

"DAD!!" The ear piercing screech made me wince as I pulled a black shirt over my head. "Get your big butt out of bed already. I'm gonna be late. Again!"

"Give me a sec!" I yelled back to my impatient son, wishing Mondays didn't exist. School shouldn't be in session on a Monday. Everyone hated Mondays, and I couldn't believe teachers hadn't lobbied for it already. And why the hell was a twelve year old boy excited about school?

I smiled as I yanked on my jeans and boots. It probably involved the cheeky little brunette cheerleader who'd been eyeing my boy at basketball practice for about a week. *A chip off the old block.* I stepped into the bathroom to comb my fingers through my red hair, the curse of my Irish heritage, which I'd passed on to Blair. Of course, my dad warned me the McMullogh DNA was strong, and the flames on the head passed down since time began. Of course, he'd failed to mention other traits I'd inherited, and I cursed him every day for my ignorance.

"Dad! You got two seconds before I take a crash course in driving!" I heard the front door open and slam.

"That boy has more of his mother in him than I like," I grumbled, thumping down the stairs and following him before he made good on his threat. Besides, I never let him out of my sight, if possible.

Most people cursed the heat wave rolling through Pahrump, Nevada, but I couldn't tell a difference from the ball busting scorchers typical of Nye County. Besides, heat meant no witches, and any day with no witches was a happy day. We steered clear of trees, since witches flocked to cool, forested areas, and you couldn't get further from that climate than the burning desert.

I climbed in the black Jeep, sitting on a six-inch lift with 35" tires, and buckled in, but I froze, having the intense feeling of being watched. I slowly scanned the street but saw no threat. Then again, there was Mr. Porter, who jogged passed us with dangerous fashion sense in his Speedo, but I chalked it up to his being comfortable in his sexuality. It might make me nauseous, but it wouldn't kill me.

Blair rolled his eyes. "For the love of god, Dad! We're late, and no one's gonna kill us. Stop scanning the block and drive." He threw his head back against the seat and added melodramatically, "Why did I end up with the most paranoid delusional father on the planet?" He groaned. "I have a science project due first period, and Diane was going to help set it up. I don't want to look like a slacker by showing up late. You're so overprotective, I'll be lucky to make it to school before first period is over!"

I couldn't help but smile. "Are you done with your bitter diatribe?" He shot me a withering glance, and I changed the subject. "So, Diane…is she the cheerleader you got a bug up your butt for? I can give you some pointers on your game."

"No!" He shivered. "You're a little too confident in your game, Dad. You haven't been on a date in like four years, and I won't remind you how that turned out. We're just friends anyway. I need a good grade on this project to get into that advanced science course this summer, and Diane is top of the class. She wanted to help me out. Was I supposed to say no? Just drop it."

He said it all a little too quickly. I'd set him up a year ago with a girl I thought he had a crush on. However, I was unaware of how many times a kid could fall on roller skates. Leaving the emergency room with a broken nose and wrist, Blair adamantly demanded I never set him up again. I couldn't blame him; the date sucked.

I sighed. "Give me a break. I didn't know

Uncle Seth set me up with a water sprite. And I had no clue you would suck at roller skating." I shook my head with a chuckle. "I should have posted the video on You Tube. You would have been famous."

He glared daggers at me. I held my hands up in surrender and offered him the Boy Scout symbol. "I promise I won't meddle. But I can't make promises about your Uncle Seth."

We pulled up to the school, and I parked. "Alright, kiddo, have a good day. And make sure—"

"That I don't talk to strangers or go off with some whack job. I'm not five anymore! Geez, cut the umbilical cord already." I stared at the kid, wishing he was still that young and not so snarky. "See you after school, Dad." He shrugged his backpack on and slammed the door.

I watched closely as he crossed the school yard and climbed the steps to the gaping front door, streaming inside with the last of the stragglers. Seth stood at the door, trying to look like a responsible vice principal. He wasn't the best choice for the students, but it kept my son under constant surveillance. He saluted me and followed Blair inside.

I admitted I might be overprotective, but then, Blair didn't understand the dangers pursuing us. If I had my way, he never would.

I stopped at the Country Café, a rustic joint with a barn theme, complete with little cow salt and pepper shakers and checkered tablecloths. Planks from an old bridge mounted the walls, and it only lacked bales of hay and actual animals. Every time I saw the couple who owned the place, I was surprised they hadn't keeled over, but I envied them. They were old and happy, and they loved feeding people. And they were good at it.

I walked in to the chimes making animal noises, something new. "Jax! Darlin', you go sit at your table, and I'll bring some bacon and eggs with my famous French toast!" Bergita hollered from across the room. "You need some more meat on those bones. You're looking kind of sickly."

I smiled and flexed my biceps. "Oh, baby, you know I look good. You just enjoy me praising your food." I gave her a wink as she turned bright red and smiled, heading to the kitchen. I was cocky about my appearance, but I knew I was built like a brick shithouse, and I didn't even have to work out. I liked flaunting it.

I settled into my favorite corner booth by the window, my mind racing. I had a lot of planning to do. We'd been here too long, but Blair was really coming out of his shell, and I just wanted my son to be happy. Seth hounded me constantly about the ticking time bomb of staying in one place, and I couldn't argue. But I was tired of moving, tired of running, and I minded far less than Blair did.

My brother's favorite phrase rattled through my brain again. "Jax, I love you, but one day, the horseshoe stuck in your ass is gonna explode, and I won't be the one to clean up the shit." My brother was a great guy, but I wondered how he managed to stifle the obscenities long enough to be around kids all day.

I could mask our energy imprints, or what you might call auras. But if you linger in a place too long, that imprint sticks in places you frequent, like a school or a café. I was strong, but with three of us, I couldn't keep it going forever. I was lucky I'd managed to keep our house sheltered this long. It could have been a beacon like a radioactive signal calling my bitch of an ex-wife to nuke the joint. My blood boiled with just the passing thought of her.

Amelia used to make my blood boil in a completely different way. She was everything to me, love at first sight. Her honey skin and dark auburn hair glowed, and she had an ass that would make any woman jealous. I'd been taken by her eyes, blue as the summer sky, and she could do things in the bedroom to make the Kama Sutra look like a children's book.

That had been long before I knew what she was. Fuck, that was before I knew what *I* was. Now, I hated the color blue, knowing those eyes were the first sign of a witch, and she'd attempted to betray me, to use our son for her own purposes.

I clenched my jaw. "Here you go, sugar. You let me know how much you enjoy this." Bergita jerked me from the Ghost of Christmas Past, and I chuckled at the twinkle in her eye and her little sashay of ancient, wide hips as she strolled behind the counter.

The aroma of the food on my plate distracted me, and I looked down, nearly drooling. I had a huge pile of thick-cut, fried bacon, four slices of French toast slathered with syrup, and three fried eggs cooked to a perfect over-easy. *Oh, yeah!* I dug in.

I rarely dwelt on the past, but today, my thoughts trailed to my ex-wife. I'd been running from her 'family' for twelve years; I couldn't ignore her existence. I hated her, and yet, I still couldn't tell Blair about her.

He knew we ran from witches, and I'd told him what they were capable of, but Blair thought his mother died giving birth. He didn't need to know his own mother was the evil mind behind our flight. But he was older, asking more questions, and each was harder to answer while keeping up the farce. I was tired of lying to my son, but how did I share the truth without breaking his heart and shattering mine all over again?

CHAPTER TWO

"Here's your bill, sweet cheeks," Bergita said, slapping the handwritten receipt on the table. She was my Ghost of Christmas Present today, snapping me out of reveries. "When are you bringing that boy of yours in again? He eats in a sitting as three elephants do in a week. It's good for business." She winked, patted my shoulder, and said goodbye, headed to her chair to read the paper. I'd miss that woman when we moved.

I put money on the table, including a generous tip; I had enough to spare, and she needed it. The McMullogh name valued at hundreds of millions, at least, made in the oil industry and multiplied through investments made with the assistance of a little angelic sixth sense. I didn't deal with the business end; that was Seth's role, and he had contacts and employees everywhere to keep things running smoothly without having to come out of hiding. I didn't understand how he did it, but it was serious talent.

Outside, I immediately felt I was being watched. I could shrug off once, but twice in such a short period confirmed it. "I hope you're one big son of a bitch. I've been itching for a good fight," I said under my breath. I fisted my hands and rounded the corner to the alley behind the café. I didn't need witnesses when I beat the shit out of someone. It would just cause a migraine and legal delays.

Halfway down the alley, I heard footsteps behind me, and I whirled, ready to strike. I stopped cold, not expecting what I saw. The woman before me might have cleared five feet in height, and her figure made my mouth dry, petite and clad like some sort of wet dream in tight jeans on a luscious ass, knee-high leather boots, and a white ribbed tank top that hugged the swell of a killer rack. Her blonde hair kinked in tight curls around her face, cut at an angle, higher in the back. I imagined how it would look after a hot night in bed.

Her jaw was narrow below full, kissable lips she pulled into a smirk as if she could read my mind, and I finally brought my gaze to her eyes. I stifled a vicious swear as she watched me under full, dark lashes with bright ocean blues. I seethed. "Turn around, or I'll send you back to your sisters in pieces." I couldn't cast spells like the witches, but I had powers of my own and had sure as hell learned how to use them.

She held up her hands in surrender. "Easy, big boy. Not everyone wants what your wife is after. I'm a friend." She was smug, snide, and had the nerve to roll her eyes at me. I wanted to give her an adjustment.

I scoffed. "Oh, fuck off! Do you really think I'm buying the shit you're selling? You should take your pretty little ass out of town and back to whatever mud hole you crawled from so I can go back to living a bright and happy life."

Her eyes flashed bright, and she closed them. When they reopened, she looked calmer, but her tone spoke the opposite. "Listen, you juiced up pigeon. Lay off the 'roids for a while. They're addling your brain. Your wife is headed here, accompanied by the entire coven, to kill you and retrieve the boy. She's not taking any more chances, and if you want to live, you have to trust me."

I thought I saw a tremble in her hands, and I could sense her fear when she mentioned Amelia. I was reminded of Seth's jab that I had the worst possible taste in women.

But my ego was a little bruised by her insult, and I needed a moment to recover. I would let her explain, and if I didn't like what she said, I'd put her out of my misery. "You obviously got your sense of style from Charmed, a bonus for you. I'll give you three minutes to tell me why you're here, how you know about my *ex*-wife's movements, and what you want in payment for the head's up." I pressed down hard on the urge to strangle her just for the hell of it. I didn't care whose side she was on; witches didn't bring out the best in me.

"That's a negative, bud. We can sit down in the sharing circle and gab, or you can grab your kid and your brother now, meet me at the edge of town in an hour, and live." She held her hands as if weighing the options. "Take your pick." With that, she turned and hurried back around the corner.

I stood debating for an instant and then ran after her. But she'd disappeared. "Fucking creepy witch." I sighed and ran a hand through my hair. I made a split second decision and pulled out my phone, locking the caps on the text bar and sending Seth, *FLY TIME. GRAB PACKAGE. MEET AT BASE.*

I fucking hated Mondays.

CHAPTER THREE

"What the fuck is going on?" Seth was on me the minute I walked through the door. "You can't just text me shit and not answer my call, you asshole!" I was sure he'd left his mind on his desk at school, and being a control freak, he was upset he wasn't in charge. In a sick way, his breakdown amused me.

"Calm down. Let me get in the house, and I'll explain. Where's Blair?" I pushed past him into the living room, regretful to leave the nice white tile, walls, and carpet with the open concept kitchen. I'd rented it furnished. It didn't make sense to buy a bunch of shit I'd just have to leave behind in a few months anyway.

I turned to Seth, who still hadn't answered. "Where the hell is Blair?"

He glared back at me, never one to back down, even when it was in his best interest. "If you'd answered your goddamn phone, you would know when I told him we were leaving town, he flew off like some banshee on the hunt. He should join the track team wherever we land. The little fucker has speed."

Shit! The day just got better and better. I had to find him before that witch discovered he was gone. If she hadn't already…

"I'll find Blair. I know where he might be. Stay and pack the shit we need, get everything together, and be ready. We're leaving this witch infested country." I opened the front door again.

Seth followed, pulling out his cell to text god knew who and get the ball rolling. "What freaked you out? And where are we going?!"

How could I wrap it all up in a nice little package to deliver it quickly? "A witch told me Amelia and her whole fucking coven are on their way. Does that sum it up?" He stopped texting, gaped at me, and squeaked something like, *oh, fuck me, we're dead.* Honestly, he was probably right if I couldn't find Blair fast.

Coming back to earth, Seth scowled. "Wait. Why was a witch warning you?"

I threw my hands up in exasperation. "I don't fucking know. She said not everyone wants what Amelia wants. I say it's a crock of shit. I don't trust the bitch, but I'm not sticking around to find out. If you see a short blonde babe in boots, shoot her. Save me the headache later." I climbed in the Jeep and revved the engine to life.

"Where are we going?" Seth yelled from the steps.

I smiled and hollered back, "Egypt!" before peeling out. Seth scowled and texted madly, and my phone buzzed in my pocket. I grabbed it and laughed, reading, *Who the fuck goes to Egypt? PS I HATE YOU*. Pissing my brother off was one of those small pleasures in life necessary on days like these.

I drove down the street toward the one place Blair would go, knowing it was the one place I never would. The small cemetery rested on the opposite side of town, built before the settlement was even a thought. Blair had always been drawn to places like it, places with great sorrow or pain. At four, he'd sit in the apple tree in the backyard all day, staring at the branches. I finally asked why he found it comforting, and he said in a hushed voice, "I come for her, Dad. She's so sad," and pointed behind him.

"Who's sad?" I asked, knowing what was there but praying my son didn't. The girl was eighteen at most, with straight brown hair, pale skin, and dark circles around her eyes. Her dead face was tear streaked, and she wore a white dress buttoned to her jaw line and stared at me, knowing I saw her, too. I didn't like it; ghosts tended to get needy once they knew you saw them.

"You see her, Dad. But you can't help her, she said. Only me." Blair listened to something I couldn't hear. I'd never heard a ghost, and I was scared shitless at the insinuation.

"What does she want help with?" I asked, failing at the attempt to ignore the raising of my flesh.

He stared at me, with an emerald and aquamarine, priceless jewels for eyes. "She wants to go home. She said I can help, but I don't know how." He hung his head, and I saw a few tears he tried to hide. I grabbed him and took him inside, deciding it was time to leave.

I'd cleared the history of every house since, but Blair found other places, like cemeteries or parks. Seth and I ignored spirits, but Blair clung to them, saying they were lonely. When he was in trouble or needed space, he'd retreat to those places; to sit and listen to whomever needed to talk. The idea freaked me out, but it calmed Blair.

I shook the memory away as I turned onto the narrow path through the cemetery. I scanned the headstones, finding Blair easily. I let out the breath I'd been holding and parked, jumping out and heading toward him with a silent thanks for his safety to whoever kept him listening.

I moved slowly, not wanting to startle him, admiring the old grave markers, so worn the names were no longer legible, the families who cared for them long gone. The colors of the graveyard provided an interesting oasis to the dull browns of Nevada, the grass lush and green from irrigation, and beautiful flowers in beds kept perfectly by city workers.

Near the back corner stood a large black marble angel that shone like hot tar in the rays of the sun. Its eyes turned to the sky with a desolate expression as he stretched his arms to the sky. I had to wonder who had died to warrant such an impressive but heart wrenching memorial. I stifled a shiver, finding my son with his back against the base of the statue, staring up at the sky with a similarly forlorn expression.

"Took you long enough, Dad. Are your powers weakening with old age or what?" he asked dejectedly, not even turning his head.

"I thought you'd like the alone time to contemplate the complications and conspiracies of the universe so you could figure out the meaning of life." I sat beside him and stretched out my legs, putting my arm around his shoulders and hoping to bring a smile to his face.

Instead, he sighed and leaned into me. "Dad, you know you're not funny, right?"

I scoffed. "Son, how could you say that? There are two undeniable truths about your old man. One, I'm fucking hilarious, and two, I'm sexy as hell." His face was hidden, but I felt his shoulders shake with silent laughter, a relief. "The cemetery's quiet today," I said, looking around, finding not a ghost in sight.

"It usually is. But it's the only place around with actual grass to sit on." He sighed again.

"Why are we leaving this time? I know you and Uncle Seth think I'm too young to know the truth, but you're wrong. I know what's out there. You guy made sure of that." He was trying to sound brave and mature, but he was so young, and I wasn't ready to reveal those dark secrets yet.

I tried to let him down easily. "I know you think you're ready for the entire load of shit, but the world's not all water sprites and friendly ghosts. There are creatures that thrive on death and sorrow, others revenge and violence. And I honestly hope you never have to learn about those things." I gazed out at nothing in particular.

Blair lifted his head, and I looked down into his grave expression. "It's about my mom, isn't it?"

His somber question had me choking on my own heart as it jumped into my throat. "Your mother died when you were born. Why would you bring her up?" I turned to brush some imaginary grass from my jeans.

He snorted. "Dad, I love you. But you and Uncle Seth are horrible liars. You never say her name. You don't seem upset about her death. I think Seth even smiles when you talk about it." I pressed my lips together in irritation at my son's observant and perceptive nature, as well as my brother's lack of propriety.

I took in a deep breath and exhaled slowly until my lungs were painfully empty. Then, I inhaled again. I'd waited long enough. It was time to tell him the truth.

"It's a long story, and we kept it from you because we love you. So promise not to hold it against us, okay?"

He hesitated, but then he nodded slowly. "I promise."

I ruffled his hair, proud of my son's courage, and began.

CHAPTER FOUR

Once upon a time, I was fifteen, Seth was thirteen, and we had parents. Then, they died. Grandfather flew them in his plane home from Hawaii, and he crashed. Seth was sick, and I'd refused to go without him, so what should have been a family trip turned into something more like a second honeymoon.

The whole incident blurred in my memory long ago, but I remembered the maid hugging us as she cried something in French.

There was an investigation, but they never found the plane, just some random body parts and shrapnel on the California shore. It was anyone's guess how the plane crashed, but no one cared. The front page news focused on what would happen to the world's richest orphans.

Aunt Agatha came to stay with us, and her witty and aloof demeanor allowed us all kinds of freedom. Life was golden until I turned sixteen and started seeing my parents floating around the house. Unlike Blair, I didn't have someone to tell me in was normal, and I wasn't innocent enough to think everyone saw ghosts, so I thought I was losing it. I finally noticed Seth cringe as our mother's apparition sat across the dinner table.

In awe, I leaned over and asked, "You can see them?"

He gave me a wide-eyed look. "See what?" His voice trembled.

I was desperate. "Come on, man! Mom's looking at you. Please, tell me you see her." If Seth saw them, I couldn't be crazy.

My brother told me with a nervous laugh, "This might sound fucked up, but I'm glad

I'm not the only one." We chuckled in mutual relief, and after that, Mom and Dad showed up less and less. It was a bit like losing them all over again.

We tried to maintain a normal life with school, sports, and friends. We perfected the art of oblivion, ignoring random ghostly appearances, and it gave us some peace, but even that was short-lived. Obviously, the McMulloghs were cursed.

***

"Your phone's ringing." I gazed down at Blair, who wore a mischievous grin as he stood. "If it's Uncle Seth, tell him I'm sorry I sort of kicked him."

I snorted and shook my head. "No wonder he was losing his shit." I yanked the phone from my pocket and shook off the Ghost of Ghosts Past so I could answer. I was blasted with my brother screaming so loud the words were distorted, and I held the phone at arm's length to protect my ears.

"What the fuck is going on, bro? Did you find

your damn kid yet?" He rapid fired questions I couldn't answer, and I made a mental note to switch his brew to decaf.

"Calm down already, you neurotic fool! Blair is safe, and we were having a father-son talk until you rudely interrupted. I'm sorry for not calling. I lost track of time…"

"Well, congrats on taking a fucking nap while I'm busting balls to get shit together so we can hightail our asses out of here per your not-so-friendly request," he interrupted. "Do you ever think maybe Brother Seth could use some R&R, a little vacation? Or that I might not have to watch my salt if you didn't raise my blood pressure to heart attack levels?"

Instead of entertaining a healthy brawl, I simply told him we were on our way home and hung up before he could draw in enough breath to start again. "Come on, Blair, before your uncle has an aneurism. I promise the history lesson's not over. We'll talk on the road, alright?"

He nodded and followed my quick stride.

"Uncle Seth needs a hobby. Or maybe a girlfriend. He's wound far too tight. When was the last time he got laid?"

I stared at my son, not quite sure what to say about his language. He rolled his eyes at me. "Don't give me that look, Dad. I was doomed from the start when it comes to language. I mean, I live with you and Uncle Seth. Did you think I was deaf to the living because I hear the dead?"

The kid's a fucking sponge. I couldn't hold it against him. I grumbled, "Point taken. Get in the damn Jeep."

He laughed as he buckled in. "It's fine, Dad. You go on living in your little bubble that says 'I'm a good parent'. I won't argue. Besides, you're not so bad, and I trust you to keep us safe."

I got a little choked up. "You're a smartass. Shut up." I tousled his hair and put the Jeep in drive.

CHAPTER FIVE

We drove back to the house in silence and arrived too soon, greeted by a maniacal Seth, shouldering two duffel bags with two more in his hands. He threw them in the back and growled, "Thanks for taking your time, ladies. I may not look like I've aged, but wait till you see the new wrinkles I grew on my balls while I waited."

Blair laughed and hopped out to collect a few things from his room, and I joined Seth in carrying the rest of the things waiting just inside the door. I grabbed a box full of canned goods and random camping staples.

"Are we pow-wowing fireside or something?" I asked.

He gave me a warning glare. "Don't talk shit to me, Jax. You're the one who said Egypt. The next flight within reasonable distance leaves Vegas tomorrow night. Unless you want to greet you know who with a smile and a wave, we're going camping." I watched him toss sleeping bags in the back and laughed.

"Alright, I give. You are much appreciated, oh, brother of mine." I slapped him on the back. "I'm just not sure this is the solution." I frowned, grabbing the last box full of kindling and matches.

But Seth shot me a cocky smile. "You two wouldn't have lasted a week without my brawn, my brains, and my charm." I punched him in the shoulder as Blair came out with a messenger bag, a backpack, and a small box.

He hopped in the back, and his face lit up. "Are we taking a camping trip?"

I should have known my boy would get excited about it. I changed the subject quickly.

"The main road out is a no-go." I silenced Seth's input on the reasoning behind that with a look. "We're headed out in broad daylight, mid-afternoon. Is there a decent road to take out?"

Seth pulled a map from his pocket with a smug expression, and I saw lines drawn in different colors, obviously coded for various situations. He pointed to a blue line. "We're going this way."

I scowled at the map, irritated. "I'm not great at reading maps, but I'm pretty sure there's no fucking road there."

"Exactly." He beamed. "Come on, Jax, use your brain. The best way to escape unnoticed isn't taking the road less traveled; it's taking the road that doesn't exist." I hated his attempt at humor. He jabbed a finger at the map again. "We're in a four-wheel drive. We'll forge a path through there and be back on the road a few miles out."

I glanced back at Blair, who was practically bouncing in his seat, anticipating the camping trip. Meanwhile, Seth tapped out some tune only he heard on his knees. Obviously, despite the dire situation, the adrenaline rush proved sufficient to keep moods light. I nodded and felt my own heart pounding. "Let's rock this shit." I backed out of the driveway, confident and content.

A half hour later, I cursed my brother and his dumbass ideas. My jaws hurt, and I thought I might have chipped a tooth. "My brain feels like it's in a blender!" Blair yelled, his voice vibrating as he held onto the roll bar for dear life. A glance in the rearview mirror showed his head bobbing like he was head-banging at a Metallica concert. Seth appeared solid enough until I noted his white-knuckled grip on the seat.

"Hey, Seth, maybe you should drive for a while." His eyes widened notably, and I sighed. "Or we could stop and set up camp." I had to yell to hear myself over the wind.

He just nodded, and I slammed the brakes and shut off the engine. I breathed a sigh of relief, relieved to end the jarring ride. Seth finally broke the silence with a chilling, quiet tone. "Don't say anything, Jax. Just…don't." He flexed his hands, trying to get blood flowing back into his fingers.

I snorted. "No worries. I'd rather eat cow shit baked twice and marinated in cat piss, but it really wasn't bad."

"You're a wicked son of a bitch," he spat through clenched teeth.

"Two peas in a fucking pod," I retorted.

I climbed out on shaky legs to stretch, and Blair jumped out behind me. We were at least off the grid. Vegas was probably another thirty or forty-five minutes out, and the landscape was sparse, the vegetation dead. It was as good a place to set up camp as any. No one in their right minds would venture into this godforsaken land, and it offered us an open view of anyone or anything coming at us.

Seth pointed to a crop of boulders a few dozen feet ahead and climbed into the driver's seat to pull the Jeep closer to it. Stretching his arms over his head to get the kinks out, Blair gave me a worried look. "What's Uncle Seth doing?"

Well, at least my brother and I still had privacy in our silent communication. I ruffled his hair. "Making us a little less visible in the open terrain." I coughed, the cloud of dust that had settled in his mop of hair hitting me in the face. "Okay, Pigpen, you need a bath."

His eyes shot arrows at me. "Great, Dad, that's good for the old ego." He pointed at me. "I'm not the only filthy one, and at least I don't stink." He shook his shirt, trying to get more of the desert off him.

I sniffed my arm pits, relieved to get a whiff of nothing funky, just deodorant, but Blair caught me and shook his head. He took off toward the Jeep as Seth parked, and I froze. There it was again. Whoever watched us was close. *Shit!* I sprinted toward my family. "Blair! Hurry up and get to Seth!" I called to my son, who never dawdled this much.

With a look of alarm, Blair bolted toward the

rock outcropping. I caught up and skidded to a halt. Seth was unloading supplies as I panted, "Someone's here. Do you feel it?"

His head snapped up, and as he concentrated, he cursed under his breath, locking eyes with me. "Shit, it's faint. I didn't feel it until I looked for it. How'd you catch it?"

"Dad's paranoid to the level of obsession," Blair piped up. "He's constantly on alert for signs of Enemy Number One." His tone was humorous, but I saw the fear in his eyes. "Who's out there, Dad?"

I shook my head. "I don't know yet, but I intend to find out." I got angry when someone messed with me, but I was livid and on the warpath when my son was in danger. He was my life and my heart, and I would kill or die to protect him. I offered Seth a feral grin, apparently venomous enough to cause him to take a step back. "Is the tranquilizer gun still under the seat?"

I ignored Blair's gaping mouth in favor of my brother's sinister smile. "Damn fucking straight! It's on the must-have list above the credit cards. 'Never leave home without it.'" He leaned across the floorboard, under the passenger seat.

Going into crisis mode, I started barking orders. "Blair, get in the floor of the back of the Jeep, and I'll cover you up with the sleeping bags." He started to argue, and I just pointed. "Trust me, son. I need you quiet and obedient."

He gave me a pointed look as he climbed into the Jeep. "I'm not going to hide forever, Dad." I appreciated his courage, knowing it was the best option when it came to how a 12-year-old would handle such a situation.

I turned to Seth. "I'm going out a bit to draw attention. Hide and wait for a clear shot. First chance you get, dart the bitch." I kept my voice low so Blair wouldn't hear.

Seth shrugged. "Clean and simple, error-proof. You make good plans, brother." He slapped my shoulder and gave me a look that spoke volumes about the beating he'd give me if I wasn't careful and searched for the best place to hide and aim.

I stared straight ahead, letting my mind see rather than my eyes. The power worked like sonar, or at least, that was the best description I had. Energy pulsed out of me and bounced back when there was a threat. In seconds, I knew where to go, and though I couldn't tell who it was based on the pulse, I had a pretty good fucking clue after the day I'd had.

I walked out in that direction, letting my senses maintain a 360-view for security, and I felt the other draw closer. The wind suddenly whipped around me, creating a wall of dust I couldn't see through, and as it died, the blond tart of a witch from the alley stood directly in front of me. I fought the urge to jump, startled, and then I fought the urge to jump and strangle her.

"Nice trick, chippie. I didn't know witches could fly without their brooms." I shoved my hands in my pockets, the most non-threatening position of engagement I could muster, needing her talking until Seth could settle his aim.

"Hilarious," she answered bitterly. "I didn't know a jackass could speak." She must not have seen Shrek, I thought, but I bit my tongue. Retorting wouldn't do me any favors.

She shook her head. "I'm not a witch, dumbass, or did that not cross your peanut sized mind?" She circled me slowly, her blue eyes vibrant in the mass of blond hair and dead, brown earth around her. "You didn't meet me like I asked, sweetheart. Are you afraid of little old me?" She made her way back in front of me, batting her lashes.

I tilted my head. "If you really expected me to show up, you're dumber than I am." As she walked behind me, I wondered what the fuck Seth was thinking, not taking the shot.

She shrugged. "I didn't expect your cooperation, which is why I followed you."

"Good to know." I was curious now, Seth taking his sweet-ass time. "So, what are you?" But before she could answer, I heard a whistle, and a little dart hit her in the chest, just above the heart. *That had to hurt.* I smiled.

She looked down, stunned, and then scowled at me. "You asshole." She wavered, and just before she collapsed on the hard, cracked ground, her eyes changed from blue to swirling gold.

CHAPTER SIX

I took a moment to let that sink in and knelt by her, lifting one eyelid to make sure I hadn't hallucinated. After all, we were in the burning desert. Sure as shit, her irises were still swirling. "Fucking freaky," I muttered as I threw her over my shoulder like a sack of rice. "Let's get you tied up before you wake up, shall we?" I slapped her ass, taking great satisfaction in that as I headed toward the boulders, her weight barely noticeable.

Seth met me halfway. "What the fuck? Did you know witches could pop out of thin air?"

I shook my head. "She's not a witch." Seth

stared at me confused, and as we closed in on our little encampment, I shifted her body into my arms and told him, "Look at her eyes."

He hesitantly checked them as I had, and jumped back. "What the hell is she? I've never seen anything like that in my life. I really don't like not knowing what the hell is tracking us through the middle of nowhere."

The last thing I needed was for him to panic. "Calm down and get the rope. We'll get answers after she's secure." He nodded and went for the rope, mumbling something I probably didn't want to hear. I had more important issues, like what to tell my son. I didn't have long to think, since Blair hopped out of the Jeep and ran to me.

"I saw everything, Dad! Uncle Seth is an awesome shot, you know. And you're totally cool and confident. But what is she? I mean, you never mentioned anything about creatures that could just beam themselves somewhere like Star Trek." He looked at her face with wide eyes. "She's a babe. Is she good or bad? If she's good, I want to keep her. Maybe she can teach us how to beam from one place to another." He was on overdrive, having diarrhea of the mouth and fawning over the woman in my arms like a puppy with a new toy. I almost looked behind him for the wagging tail.

"Blair, go gather some dead cactuses to start the fire." He looked hurt, but I was tired, and I couldn't think fast enough to answer his questions. Would this day ever end?

He walked away dejectedly, his head hanging as he kicked at the dirt. I would have to apologize for being short. I sighed and tossed the woman back over my shoulder, patting the luscious ass by my head again. "Well, m'lady, shall we?" I chuckled. I was fucking hilarious.

Seth stood by the Jeep, rope in hand, and I dumped the limp body unceremoniously by the front tire. The chick was a thorn in my side. A couple of physical bruises weren't any more dangerous than her bruised ego. "Tie her to the front bumper. We can just drive it into the boulders if she turns out to be a demon," Seth said with a shiver. He grabbed her feet and dragged her, sitting her up and wrapping the ropes around her.

I didn't argue. "I'm gonna help Blair set up a fire. She should be out for a while, but stay with her just in case."

"Sure, Jax. I'll stay with Miss Freaky Eyes and dart her again if she gets belligerent." I pictured him sitting four feet in front of her with the gun pointed at her chest all night, waiting for a chance to pop her again.

I found Blair and started grabbing the dead vegetation to add to the box he was filling. We worked silently for a bit, and I finally stood and wiped my brow. "Look, bud, I'm sorry for my attitude. It's been a long day, and I shouldn't take it out on you. Can you forgive your crazy old man?"

He gave me a small smile. "Sure, Dad." He thought for a second and added, "You still owe me the rest of the story. No more interruptions." As if to force the issue, he walked over to a shaded area beneath a large cactus and sat in the dirt.

I shrugged. "Fair enough." I flipped the box over, not caring if the contents spilled, and used it as a seat. I raked a hand through my hair, raining dust all over myself, and thought about where to pick back up.

***

Other strange things started happening, like clearer night vision, unusual strength and speed. Coach Peen was shocked at Seth's ability in wrestling, having considered him a puny weakling. The day he faced off with Coach and had him pinned with one hand in 2.8 seconds changed people's perception of us, and they started treating us like aliens. Truthfully, we didn't fit in anymore.

One afternoon, when Seth needed a ride to the dentist, I waited more than twenty minutes in the parking lot as it emptied, pacing around the car, impatient and worried. People were late all the time, but I felt lightheaded, and anxiety clutched at my chest.

I checked inside, thinking he'd gotten caught

up in a discussion with a teacher, or maybe sitting in detention for his smart mouth again. But as I stepped toward the school, the world seemed to move in slow motion. Heightened awareness showed me a rabbit behind a boulder to my left, a couple of kids in the locker room getting hot and heavy, and Seth, amidst a group gathered on the south side of the school.

I booked it around the building, finding Seth surrounded by the entire football team. This was not going to end with sunshine and rainbows. I stayed back, and as I imagined the various things my baby brother could have done to wrangle himself into such a situation, I heard his voice. "I didn't realize you all still needed a date to the spring formal. Why don't you line up, and I'll choose the best kisser to take me along."

I winced and crouched down, waiting to see how he was going to talk himself out of this mess.

"Tell us why you're so fucking weird, nerd." That from the gnarly looking team captain,

Danny. The guy was large enough to swallow a cow and ask for seconds. The others nodded agreement. *A horde led by the village idiot.* They might as well be carrying pitchforks and torches. I cursed my brother.

Seth had the nerve to smirk at him. "That's simple. I'm a superior, cognitively developed, intellectually gifted individual. It allows me to function on a significantly higher level than the average human, and it causes me to be a conundrum for those who can't achieve even an average level of intellect. Would you like me to repeat that for you, you ignorant piece of excrement?"

The horde exchanged blank looks, blushing and growing irritated at not understanding of the insult they knew they'd received. I stood and brushed off, ready to throw a couple of punches in my brother's defense.

But a slender arm shot out, and thin fingers yanked me back. I glared at her, shocked and angry, but I was speechless as I stared at an exotic, dark complexion set with bright blue eyes. She was stunning, and I wanted her.

Natasha Dawn

CHAPTER SEVEN

"Let a lady handle this," she said in a heavy southern accent that rolled over my skin and gave me goose bumps. She wore a white sundress that left little to the imagination and a gold necklace with a tiny pearl dove pendant that changed colors in the sunlight. She was a masterpiece as she approached the group of mutants with a swagger that made trees bow to her. "Hey, boys! I just got into town. Who wants to show me around?"

With tongues dragging the ground, the Neanderthals practically climbed over each other, clambering for her attention. She gave me a wink and headed around the other side of the school, the football team on her heels like coyotes. I would have been just as mindless if I hadn't worried about my brother, who had almost become dog food.

As she disappeared from view, my head cleared, and I wasn't sure if she was real or a wet dream. "Get out of the bushes, creeper," my brother called as he jogged toward me. "Tell me you weren't jacking off to the scene of the Great Seth McMullogh about to destroy the entire defensive line."

I barely registered offense. "You know, Seth, we may be a little stronger than average, but no way were you going to take on the whole damn team. What the hell were you thinking?" I punched his arm; still staring at the last place I'd seen the angel. "Do you know that girl?"

He didn't answer, and I glanced at him to find a quizzical and somewhat concerned look on his face. "What girl?"

"The one who just saved your scrawny ass, Seth. How could you miss her?"

His mouth made an 'oh'. "You mean the slutty anorexic chick with the 'look at me' complex. Jax, don't tell me you think she's hot. You know who she reminds me of? That alien in the movie we just watched who ate her boyfriend from the penis up."

I rolled my eyes, walking away. "She's not an alien. You should be grateful. She just saved your life." I couldn't get her out of my head. I had to have her. Seth sneered at me in disgust.

"You have the worst taste in women. That chick's going to be the death of you."

"Stop being so negative and get in the car. We're late for your appointment, and Aunt Agatha's going to be pissed." As I started the engine, Seth grew quiet and distant.

Finally, he asked quietly, "What are we, bro? Why are we different?"

I didn't have an answer. We were some kind of human, or so I had to believe. I sighed and turned onto the road. "I don't know, Seth."

There was only a month left of school; I'd been chomping at the bit to get out of town and start over somewhere else, but as I walked into school the next day, I searched in vain for her face in the crowd. As Seth and I headed out for the afternoon, she stood in jean shorts and a yellow tank top, leaning against the driver's side door like some pin-up girl.

She smiled at me, and the sun shone from her lips. "I thought maybe you'd give me a ride home, big boy."

Her eyes captivated me, but Seth scoffed. "No, he wouldn't. Get your dirty ass off our car and out of our lives."

I shot daggers at him. "Calm down, and be polite." I turned back to her. "I sure as hell wouldn't leave a lady all alone. Hop in…" I arched a brow in question.

"Amelia Estelle," she said. I took her offered hand and nearly fell to my knees. "I'm right outside of town. Thanks for the ride."

Seth grumbled in the back seat, and I thought I heard the word *freeloader*, but I chose to ignore him. Before she climbed in, he leaned forward and told me, "I warned you, Jax.

When she bites your head off after you bang her, I'm not going to mourn your suicide."

I should have listened to the wisdom I'd been sure my brother lacked.

CHAPTER EIGHT

"My mother's name was Amelia." Blair squinted into the hot sun as it lowered toward the horizon.

"I'm sorry, son. Some things are better forgotten." Gazing down at him, he looked much older than twelve, his jaw line strong and the puffy baby cheeks angling into those of a man. "You're growing up faster than I'm prepared for." I rested my elbows on my knees and stared into the sunset.

He made a disgusted noise. "Don't get all sappy." He looked up at me, like he was seeing me for the first time. "I guess it's okay to have secrets to protect someone."

I smirked to cover the wave of emotions crashing over me. "Who's getting sappy?" I squeezed his shoulder lightly. "You're a good kid, Blair, growing into a strong man." I stood and offered a hand, pulling him to his feet.

"I guess you haven't done so bad raising me after all," he joked, picking up the spilled cactus and putting it back in the box. "You can finish later. It's gonna get cold fast."

He was right, and as we headed back, I caught sight of Seth, still sitting in front of our captive audience, the gun resting on his knee. I also noted quickly she wasn't out anymore but staring at him, obviously enraged. Seth gave me a weary look. "It's about time. Freak over here woke up about three minutes after I finished tying her up."

He poked her with the gun, eyes blazing, and she kicked out at him, barely missing his knee. "Has she said anything?" I asked.

"Not a word." Seth stood and stretched, but the woman's foot shot out like lightning, knocking him to the ground. In a heartbeat, she had his neck between her shins, ready to twist, and I lunged for the dart gun.

"Apologize, dick weed, before I snap your neck." She looked up at me with a smirk. "I might be willing to leave the world to its fate, just to silence this asshole."

His face was turning purple, and he finally gave a short nod, gasping for air when she released him. He scurried away, and I kept my distance, gun in hand. I shook my head. "That was fun. Are we ready to talk like civilized beings?" I asked, pushing Blair behind me protectively as he stepped forward.

"Who are you?" Blair asked, poking his head around me.

The woman stood, shaking off the ropes, and I glared at Seth, deciding never to trust him with a rope again. "My name is Seraphina," she said as she moved into the shade, grabbed one of our water bottles, and plunked down cross-legged. She poured the water over the back of her neck, and three men were silenced as it ran down the valley between her breasts. I blinked to clear the unwelcome arousal and tried to focus.

"Okay, Finney, what he fuck are you doing following us, and what the hell are you?" I probably should have asked one question at a time, but I was angry and stunned, and I needed answers. She glared at me, and I rolled my eyes. "I apologize for not being more accommodating, but you seem to know a lot about our situation, and you can't really blame me."

She gazed back at me with narrowed eyes and seemed to be talking to herself. "Finney? I've never been called that before. I don't like it. No, you may not call me Finney." She stood and addressed me. "I apologize for surprising you earlier. You are correct, and as a fellow warrior, I commend you for your discretion."

I'd prepared for battle and was thwarted by the sudden about-face. Rendered speechless, all I could do was stare as she continued, "As for what I am…" She gave a grand smile and twirled, disappearing into a swirl of sand. She reappeared suddenly behind Seth and whispered, "I am an Air Elemental."

"What the fuck?!" Seth jumped out of his skin and landed in a shuddering heap of bones four feet away. He turned the gun on her, but she was already gone. I grabbed Blair by the wrist and pressed him between me and the rocks, wondering if I'd catch a long enough break from the unexpected to get rid of my throbbing headache.

"Relax, boys," her voice sounded fluttery out of nowhere. "I'm here to help, not harm." She showed up six feet away, hands in the air. "I could have gotten out of your ridiculous rope at any time to attack, and yet, I didn't. At least offer me a modicum of trust."

Her smile looked like the Cheshire cat as she seated herself on the ground, her legs folded, and the sun behind her blond hair cast an otherworldly halo around her face. It was mesmerizing, and the only dulling effect was the reminder in the back of my mind of the last time I'd had such a reaction to a woman.

"Okay, enough fancy tricks, Finney," I said with a smirk, watching her nose wrinkle in revolt. "Tell me what an 'air elemental' is and why you want to help us."

She tilted her head at me with what I could only call a seductive smile. "I'll tell you my story if you finish yours…"

In the fading light, the tiny specks of silver in her eyes sparkled like glitter. The breeze kicked up and fluttered her hair, and the scent of the ocean on a cool night swept over me. I inhaled deeply and asked, "What story are you talking about?" I was puzzled by her question, and more confused by my physical reaction to her.

She rolled her eyes. "The one you've been telling your son."

How did she know…

I was an idiot. She'd admitted to following us. She must have been listening the whole time. Her laughter tinkled around me. "I am the air, my friend, and I can hear every word spoken if I choose to listen."

Blair pushed out from behind me, my grasp on him loosened in my complete awe. "The story about my mother," he said with certainty.

"You told him?" Seth said accusingly.

I shrugged. "He wanted to know, and he's ready for the truth. He's old enough now." I gazed at Serendipity or whatever her name was. "I'll tell my story in my own time. I don't have time for your bullshit. I need an explanation right now. If you're telling the truth, Amelia could be here, roasting us over a bonfire any…" Seth inhaled sharply, and I stopped, realizing what I'd just said.

I looked quickly at Blair, whose shocked expression was enough confirmation he hadn't missed a beat. "My mother's alive? Dad, you told me she died!"

I knelt quickly and looked into his pale face, trying not to cringe. "Remember your promise, son. You said you wouldn't judge or hold anything against me." But the look on his face broke my heart. "I didn't want you to find out this way, Blair. I swear, I wouldn't have lied to you if there wasn't more to the story."

He just stared at me, and I called over my shoulder, "Seth, set up the fire. It's going to be a long night." I eyed the 'elemental' meaningfully. "We've all got a lot to talk about."

CHAPTER NINE

"Are you gonna stare at the fire all night, or are you gonna tell me the rest of it?" Blair's voice was irritated and demanding, and considering the way our new addition to the group had spilled the beans, I couldn't blame him. I was just having trouble getting my tongue to work.

I tossed a rock toward the fire, making the embers crackle as it hit. "Amelia teased me all through high school, and I couldn't let her go. Your Uncle Seth is not a wise man, but in this case, I should have listened to him. He always told me she was trouble brewing."

"Damn straight! Brother, you have the worst—"

"Taste in women, I know," I finished for him, cutting him off. I didn't miss the smirk on Serengeti's face. Or whoever she was. "Anyway, I was obsessed, and I did anything and everything she asked of me. I felt indebted to her for saving Seth's scrawny ass, and she was just so perfect I couldn't take my eyes off her."

"Witches have glamour," the woman interrupted, and I stared at her, unappreciative of her interruption but also curious how she knew so damn much about witches. She added, "Witches may create an image of themselves in a man's head that is equal to their actuality but also more appealing in nature."

That was as clear as a bog in Louisiana on a rainy day. I shook my head and went on. "Finally, just before graduation, we got together, and she told me she loved me. I proposed, and life as I knew it was over." I rested my elbows on my raised knees and ran a hand through my hair. "We didn't have to worry about money, and I bought a house, moved us in. She…treated me well." I heard Seth stifle a chuckle, and I shot him a warning look. I didn't want to discuss my sex life with Amelia while addressing our son. "For about four months, everything was grand. We were going to wait a while to have kids."

Blair's face fell. "Did she leave because she didn't want me?"

"No, son, it's not like that at all. Your mother is a witch, and they don't form the same bonds with their families as the rest of us do. She had a different purpose for you, which is why she got pregnant despite us having agreed otherwise. I was a little shocked and didn't handle it well at first, and that's when she showed her true colors. She put thoughts in my head, avoided me like the plagued, addressed me like a fucking piece of gum on the bottom of her Prada shoes.

"She didn't know I'd been listening into her coven meetings. I didn't understand at first; they were supposedly life coaches or something like that. Mentors, that's what she called them. But the more I listened, the more I realized I had to get you out of there at the first opportunity."

"You never did tell me exactly what you overheard," Seth grumbled from his spot, leaning against the rocks. I glanced at him, and then I let my eyes roam the circle. Blair sat forward, looking devastated and anxious, and the 'elemental' stared at me with wide eyes and rapt attention. I had to look away from her; her eyes glowed almost as bright as the fire, and while it was creepy, it was also intoxicating.

"I don't remember everything. But I do know that Amelia chose me for a reason. Her coven meant to fulfill a prophecy, stating the offspring of a fallen angel and a witch would supply entrance to heaven. I still don't know a lot about this fallen angel thing, but I heard enough to know that Seth and I are both of that lineage, which explains a lot of strange things that have happened to us in the past." I locked eyes with Blair. "You, son, are the key, and they will do anything to get their hands on you. If they take you, they won't care what happens to you once you've fulfilled their purpose."

"How can I be a key?" Blair asked, confused and hurt. I knew this was going to be hard for him, but I still felt there should be a way to ease his pain.

"I don't know, Blair. All I know is that they'd use you to open the way to heaven, and I can't imagine that being a good thing. And once you'd served your purpose, they would kill you so no one else could get in. That's why I've watched over you so closely, and that's why we have to keep running. Blair, your mother isn't dead, but she's dead to me. She betrayed me and planned a horrible fate for you. And as much as it hurts to say this, we would be better off if she was dead."

I watched my son's face and felt tears threaten my own eyes at the utter dejection expressed in his. I didn't move toward him because I felt like Enemy Number One right now, so Seth scooted closer and draped an arm around his shoulders. "Your mother is purely evil, Blair, and we only wanted to protect you."

Seth wasn't a particularly sensitive guy, but I appreciated his recognizing the appropriate times to wear the mask. "Amelia is a pawn." I turned to look at our guest, stunned, and I saw Blair and Seth do the same from the corner of my eye. She bore holes right into me as she spoke. "There are greater forces at work than the witch Amelia, and she is merely a means to an end, much like Blair."

Seth moved quickly, grabbing the tranquilizer gun and leveling it at her. "Now, listen carefully. That bitch used my brother and wants to use my nephew like some piece of metal. I don't care if she's possessed by the devil himself. She doesn't get a free pass."

"Of course not. Only someone with evil intentions could be swayed to follow a course dominated by such evil." She seemed unaffected by my brother's threat, speaking in an even tone.

I seethed and wished I could grab Blair and

run, leaving Seth to duel it out with her. Instead, I told her, "You better explain that fast, before I blow a gasket."

She smiled sympathetically. "I have followed you long enough to know your parents told you nothing of your heritage. You had no idea of what you were begotten until your *ex*-wife happened to inadvertently slip some of the information to you. That is unfortunate. However, witches such as Amelia can sense such things, and she knew the moment she first came into your life you were fallen angels."

"Wait a minute," Seth said, waving an arm wildly in the air. "First of all, I haven't fallen from anywhere. And I sure as fuck don't feel like an angel. This is the biggest crock of horseshit I think I've heard in my life, and believe me, I've heard some good ones."

"Shut up, Seth," I finally snapped. "I know the term, but he's right. How does it apply to us? We were born here, on earth. Weren't we?"

The elemental, whose name I was going to have to learn, tilted her head in consideration. "Perhaps it makes more sense to say you and your brother are the offspring of fallen angels. Therefore, you were born on earth but possess many but not all of the same powers of an angel. For example, Jax, your sense of being watched, your incredible strength and speed, and ability to shelter your auras. And Seth, you are able to see the dead like your brother, are a genius with numbers, and are far more agile than the average human."

Seth glared at me. "Why didn't you say something before?"

I shrugged. "What good would it have done? It didn't really make sense to me. I figured it was probably easier to go about business as usual and just learn to use our talents for the better. It's not like we ever had time or opportunity to really look into it." He continued to stare me down, and my jaw clenched. Through my teeth, I told him, "All I learned from my ex-bitch was that she needed a child with the blood of a fallen angel and a witch so the coven could open the gates to heaven. She chose me for that reason. I already told you most of that."

Seth ran a hand down his face like he was scrubbing it, and I turned back to our current orator. "Okay, we'll talk about those implications later. Right now, I want to know more about whoever or whatever you say is bigger and badder than Amelia."

"Azazel." The one word, for some reason, made my blood run cold. I shivered, despite the heat of the fire. I waited, and she continued, "Azazel is the original fallen angel, who coerced several others to follow him to earth and marry human women. They were the creators of the Nephilim, the most sinful of beings, and he taught the art of false beauty. He was cast into Duduael, a pit in the desert that was to be his prison for eternity, bound and sentenced to lie upon jagged rocks in complete darkness with his face covered. He was chained there, and when man's sin was paid with the sacrifice of the Christ, God determined that, on the Day of Judgment,

Azazel would be cast into the fire and cease to exist."

"I've heard that story," Blair whispered, his face a mask of terror.

The elemental nodded, and I couldn't look away from her as she continued to tell the story, her face animated and highlighted all the more by the light of the flames that flickered and shifted in the wind. "The race of witches is the descendants of those who learned magic from him, and they have sought to free Azazel for many centuries. While he is still chained and tormented, they have provided him with a means by which to see once again. He is the one who put these events in motion, for he convened with the witches of Amelia's coven and told them of the prophecy."

Even Seth was enraptured, and in a voice filled with awe, he asked, "Are you saying he's ruling over these heinous bitches that are always on our heels?"

"I am telling you precisely that. Amelia is a

lost cause, as are the others in her coven. They believe, once they have opened the gates to Heaven with your son, Azazel will seek revenge on the angels who still reside there and allow Amelia and her coven to rule from on high. In actuality, he intends to destroy them and usurp the power for himself."

"He wants to become god," I stated plainly. Her lack of response answered me, and I shivered again. I could imagine the apocalypse that would ensue if he succeeded, and I fixed my gaze on my son, my fury turning his skin a shade of red as I thought about losing him to such a terrible purpose. "If he succeeds, we won't be the only ones who suffer."

"I have sworn to protect the heavens with my life force," the elemental added with an air of gravity. Her eyes no longer shone, and I could almost feel her heavy heart weighing on my chest. "We can thwart the plan, but we must be prepared. Azazel's time grows short, and his impatience grows strong. He will not rest until he succeeds, and therefore, we must make haste."

"Make haste at what?" I asked, getting to my feet and starting to pace. "Are we supposed to prepare for a war with the coven? Or maybe we're supposed to destroy an angel that can only die at the hands of god or another angel. Both sound like suicide missions to me. So, why are we in a hurry again?"

"We must open the gates first," she told me, and I halted mid-step. I gaped at her, and she beamed in triumph. "The prophecy is well known among my kind, and it states that, once a key has opened the gates to Heaven, it is no longer viable. If we reach the gates with Blair, and he opens them, he can then shut them, and he will never again be able to open the gates. He will be useless to Azazel and the witches, and their plan will fail."

It was brilliant. I couldn't believe how simple that was. I wanted to believe that, if I'd known that small detail, I could have saved us all a great deal of trouble much sooner, but I would never know. Right now, I was stoked, and I wanted to pack up the Jeep and leave right away.

But Blair's small voice brought me back to reality. "How are we going to reach the gates to Heaven?" he asked, his worried gaze fixated on our guest.

She smiled and reached over to brush a hand over his hair, which glowed with the same color as the flames. "There are portals in many places on earth. The nearest to us is a two-day drive. We must reach the portal so you can open and close the gates before your mother and her coven gets to you."

I strode to my son, pulling him to his feet and pulling him into a fierce hug. "I told you there were evil things in this world I didn't want you to meet. If we get this done, I don't think you'll ever have to worry about those evil things again."

He didn't respond, and I knelt in front of him, searching the brave front he put up to find the absolute horror beneath. In a tiny voice I hadn't heard since he was about five, he told me, "I'm scared, Dad. I'm never scared, but this scares me. It's a really big responsibility, like, the whole world depends on me."

What was I supposed to say? He was right, but I didn't want to add to the pressure. At the same time, I'd already promised I was done lying to him. "You're a tough kid, Blair, far more mature than I've been giving you credit for. I trust you, son. We can do this, and then there will be no more running, no more hiding. If you want, we can even come right back to Nevada so you can get your game on with that pretty little cheerleader you like, whether you want to admit it or not."

He stood there, with the weight of humanity – and the Heavens – on his shoulders, and I saw the moment his determination took over. He squared his shoulders and held his head up. With the bravest face I'd ever seen on a child, Blair turned to our new ally and asked, "When do we start?"

CHAPTER TEN

I was awake with the first ray of sun as it peered like a laser beam over the horizon, and I had everyone else on their feet in short order. Seraphina – whose name I'd finally committed to memory – helped me load the Jeep, and while I poured over the map with Seth, helped Blair erase the traces of our fire.

I could hear the laughter and bantering between them, and I felt the pang of regret that Blair never had a real mother, the kind to hold him and read to him, rock him to sleep at night, to sing to him when he was sick. I'd done my best, but I couldn't fill in for two parents, and Seth certainly wasn't capable of feminine care and comfort.

I scowled at the route Seth had marked on the map, scratching my head. He pointed to the destination, which Seraphina had kindly provided. "This is about 1700 miles away, no matter what roads we take. We're talking about driving 14 hours a day for two days to get there, and that's if we don't have any stops along the way."

I doubted we'd manage that, so I mentally adjusted the time to three days. "Tell me those marks leading to it don't require us to shake our brains until the fucking liquid pours out of our ears."

He shrugged. "If you could read a damn map, maybe you could do better. But you can't, so I guess you'll have to fucking trust your baby brother for once. We can be out of this hell hole in about twenty minutes if we turn south and find the road, and then it's smooth sailing from there."

"Assuming we don't have rainbow fireballs

blasting the Jeep and turning it into a giant circus car or blowing up like a nuclear bomb," I reminded him. "Are these main roads? I don't know if I can shield us moving as fast as we need to."

Seth glanced back at Seraphina and Blair who were now chanting some sort of rhyme together. Quietly, he said, "I don't know about you, but I think her energy is more potent than ours. Maybe it'll help hide us, like muddling the scent so a bloodhound can't find the rabbit."

He had a point; Seraphina was a very strange entity, and while I still didn't quite understand *what* she was, and I wasn't ready to give her my full trust, I felt her power surrounding us, like a breath of fresh air. I made a face at my own description of the air elemental, not a fan of puns. "Okay, but if we're attacked, I'm blaming you."

"That's fair." He closed the map and looked me dead in the eye. "We're taking Crazy Eyes with us, aren't we?"

I turned around and watched Seraphina and Blair, sparring in a high-energy boxing match. She was so light on her feet she almost didn't seem to touch the ground as she feinted back and forth, laughing and teasing with my son. Blair had taken to her well, and I found her incredibly intriguing, as well as easy on the eyes. She had more information I wanted, I was certain of that. And at least if she was a lying sack of shit, taking her along would mean keeping the enemy close. "Yes, we're taking her, and I don't want to hear you bitch or moan or question my judgment in women this time."

He held up his hands in surrender. "Hey, she's not a witch, and that right there is an upgrade for you." I gave him a warning glare, and he chuckled. "I know, it's not like that. But tell me you wouldn't want to see just how acrobatic she is in the bedroom."

"Not the time or place for this discussion," I growled and walked away before I got myself in some serious trouble. I approached Blair, but my eyes rested on the elemental. She smiled at me, her golden eyes swirling and sparkling, and her blond hair slightly less curly and bouncy today. I wondered if she changed her appearance on a daily basis. "Hey, boy, are you ready to rock?"

Blair nodded. "I'm ready. Where exactly are we going?"

I shook my head in disbelief of the irony. All this time, I'd been avoiding forests, water, and places known for drawing the supernatural and the nasty things of the world. Now, we were heading straight into snake pit. "It's time to get some Cajun food, Blair. We're going to New Orleans."

***

I hadn't been back to Flagstaff since before I'd married, and even nearing the city brought back memories. Home, high school, my parents, Aunt Agatha. We'd lived in Prescott, about an hour and a half south of Flagstaff, and as we stopped for gas and a bathroom break after more than four hours on the road, I stretched and looked around at how things had changed, feeling nostalgic.

"We're awfully fucking close to home," Seth said, sidling up beside me as I pumped gas. Seraphina had tagged along with Blair, who'd insisted on snacks for the road, and they were inside, probably tossing candy bars at each other. They'd done little but laugh and talk for the last 260 miles.

"You caught that, did you?" I asked sarcastically. I started looking over my shoulder, scanning the area, feeling something not quite right. "I don't like being here. It's not safe."

"So, we'll fill her up, pack up the kid and the nymph, and hightail it the fuck out of here."

It sounded simple enough, but I had a feeling it was already too late. I heard the rest of our traveling band approaching as I hung up the nozzle, and as I turned to watch them, my gaze landed on a figure in the distance, standing by the corner of the store, watching me intently. Her hair was white-blond, and I didn't need to get any closer to see the sky blue of her eyes.

"Get in the Jeep, now," I barked at Seth. I reached for Blair as he reached me and practically shoved him in the back seat. Seraphina's eyes grew wide, and she instantly picked up on the issue, turning to stare right at the witch. "Let's go!" I hollered.

She was in the car faster than I could finish yelling, and I jumped in the passenger seat as Seth floored it out of there. "Where am I going?" he asked as I fumbled with the seat belt and checked to make sure Blair had his on.

"I don't know!" Arizona was full of desert, but if they'd already tracked us, there wasn't much we could do to lose them.

Seraphina leaned forward, and I realized she wasn't buckled in. Of course, if we had an accident, I was sure she could just swirl away like a tornado, and it pissed me off to think she could save herself when we were all powerless. "Leave the path we're foraging," she said, and I looked at her, trying to figure out what the hell she was talking about. "We don't want them to determine the direction we're heading or why. If they figure out our destination too soon, we will never make it to the portal before them."

I knew of two places within driving distance we could go to lead them astray, and I wasn't up for driving all the way to Phoenix, a three hour trip each way, with a horde of angry, desperate witches on our tail. That only left…

"You know, Seth, maybe it's time for the prodigal sons to return."

He groaned. "Are you sure?" I nodded, resigned to the fact that, likely, fate had forced our hands. "Okay, then. Mr. Sulu will set a course for Prescott."

CHAPTER ELEVEN

It was early afternoon as Seth pulled up to our childhood home in Prescott. He'd taken some back roads, and we'd somehow evaded capture or even a skirmish with the witch and her flock of Broom-Hildas. I swallowed my heart as it jumped into my throat as I faced the manor house for the first time since I'd graduated high school. I thought I'd never come back, but life has a way of keeping us all from being permanently content.

"Whoa!" Blair gasped from the back seat. "Dad, you and Uncle Seth grew up here? How come we've never gotten a house like this?"

I'd been impressed when I was twelve, too. The house sprawled out over 5,000 square feet, with another couple thousand on the second floor. The landscapers were apparently still getting paid because the lawn was perfectly green, even in this godforsaken desert, and the shrubs were perfectly trimmed. I imagined all the little trinkets and antiques and collectibles inside were dusted and polished as well.

Seth shut off the engine, and I stepped out, reluctant to go inside, but Blair was already running toward the door, and I scanned the horizon to make sure we were alone, not thrilled at the prospect of chasing him down. I wasn't twelve now, and I didn't have a constant source of renewable energy.

Seraphina came around to me and told me quietly, "Blair is a wonderful child. Even in your continuous flight, you have done an excellent job as a parent. He seems well adjusted under the circumstances, and quite happy in most aspects of his life."

I didn't answer, feeling a little too emotional

at finally getting some sort of validation, even if it was from some sort of magical creature. In a more serious voice, she said, "You, however, seem tortured. Your breath comes in heavy sighs, labored, and here, it is worse than I've seen it before. You are haunted by your childhood memories because you never understood your unusual powers. I believe your parents intended to explain it to you at the age of maturity and were simply denied that opportunity."

"Right. A shit ton of good it does for me to think that now, when I still only know enough to be a danger to myself." I was angry all over again, and I rounded on her in my rage. "You heard how I met Amelia. My brother nearly got himself killed because he was testing the boundaries of our strength. He was a fourteen year old junior because he was so intellectually advanced. And we were both convinced we were insane, traumatized by our parents' deaths, because we can see dead people. But it gets better because my poor son fucking talks to the god damned ghosts, and I could never even tell him if it was normal or not."

I was on a rant, and Seraphina just stood there, silent and calm, and listened. It took the gusto out of me, and I seemed to shrink a bit. She opened her mouth, made an 'oh', and blew a light, cool wind at me. It was scented of lavender and chamomile, and I inhaled deeply, closing my eyes as everything within my body relaxed.

When it stopped, I peered at her, amazed. "How did you do that?"

"I told you, I am an air elemental. I am the life in the air, and the air is my life force." Saying no more, she bounced off toward the front door, which Seth was promptly unlocking while Blair shifted from one foot to the other in anticipation. I, personally, was distracted by the sway of the fairy's hips, the curve of her ass, and the way her hair bounced with her.

Shaking it off, I jogged to catch up with the group just as they stepped inside.

So many things had changed outside, but inside, it was like a museum. Aunt Agatha had moved into an assisted living community when we'd graduated, and not a single thing in this house had changed since. The chandelier in the foyer twinkled, the lights glinting off the gold frames around family portraits. I didn't have to go any further to know the rest would be the same.

"I'm not sleeping in my old room," I grumbled, and Seraphina seemed to be the only one who heard. She turned and arched a brow at me, as if to insinuate I was acting childish. I sucked it up and headed toward the kitchen, where I could hear my son opening and closing cupboards. He stared at the industrial sized fridge as I entered, giggling. "Are you impressed, kiddo?" I asked.

Blair grinned at me. "Come on, Dad, this is a palace. I can't believe you left this place!"

"I couldn't keep you here."

Blair rolled his eyes. "I don't think you married my mom and moved in here, with Aunt Agatha, Dad. I have to tell you how stupid you must have been to give all this up for some hot chick who blew you off for almost two whole years."

"I don't think this is the right time to rag on your dad, okay?" I winced internally, knowing he was right. At the same time, I couldn't imagine life without Blair, and that was enough reason for me. "Come on, let's make use of these appliances and make some food. I'll get some of the supplies out of the Jeep so we can cook. You stay inside, alright?"

He rolled his eyes, apparently his favorite response these days, and said, "Fine. I'll wait here." I hurried out to the Jeep and came back with a box of the canned and sustainable goods. I wanted something better, but this was what we had, and I would make it work. I just didn't trust that my son would stay in the house if I was gone too long.

I found pots and pans still stashed in the same cabinets they'd been in when I was a kid, and Blair and I worked together to try to make something edible out of cans of vegetables, chili, and soup. It eased some of my stress to hear him joke and laugh, as he'd been doing with Seraphina.

It prompted me to ask, "What do you think of our little air friend?"

He didn't look at me. "I think she's nice. I mean, she has some scary magic stuff going on, but if you're worried she's evil, I don't think she is. She's a lot of fun and has a really interesting sense of humor. I guess, other than watching us, she hasn't had a lot of experience with humans."

I started to correct him and tell him we weren't exactly human. Then again, some of the most mundane people I knew didn't quite pass as human, either. "So, are you teaching her all the ins and outs? You were talking a lot." I didn't want to probe too much, but I admittedly was a little jealous of what seemed to be a blooming friendship.

"Sort of, I guess. We're kind of trading information. She told me about the history of witches and about the different kinds of elementals, and I taught her some slang and stuff like that."

I wondered exactly what 'stuff like that' was,

but Seth and Seraphina both emerged at the same time from different parts of the house, and we sat down to eat – using the good china Aunt Agatha had never let us use.

It was a quiet meal, and I think everyone else was as lost in thought as I was. When we finished, Seraphina cleared the table, putting all the dishes in the sink. I followed her into the kitchen, and she frowned at the pile of plates. "I would wash them, but I'm afraid I might hurt the china."

I waved it off. "The maid's going to freak out because we're never here, but she'll take care of it."

But Seraphina wasn't listening. I scowled, seeing her eyes swirling as she tilted her head in every direction. I couldn't figure out what she was doing, especially as she moved past me, as if someone was calling her and she followed the sound. Only, I couldn't hear it. Curious and a bit disturbed, I trailed behind her as she almost floated through the dining room, into the foyer, and back to the library. She walked the perimeter of the library, and I stood in the middle of the room, watching.

Eventually, she tiptoed gracefully over to the large oak desk and placed her ear to the surface. By that point, I was losing my mind. "What the hell are you doing?" I blurted out.

"Hush," she whispered, tapping her nails along the polished top. She stood, looking confounded. "There's a whistling, and it's coming from here."

"Whistling?" What the fuck was she talking about? I turned to Seth and Blair, who now stood in the doorway, but Seth didn't seem to have a clue, and Blair just watched with interest.

"When air comes through a small space, it whistles. You probably would not hear it with your ears, but as an air elemental, even the slightest shift in the air is notable to me from a great distant. I heard it in the kitchen." She met my eyes and asked, "Can we move this desk?"

I stepped forward to help her, but apparently, she didn't need help and was only asking permission. I stood frozen as she called up a gust of air that lifted the desk, floated it to the side, and settled it on the hard wood floor again without a scratch. I scowled as she slid the rug beneath it aside and uncovered something that had me staring straight into Seth's similarly shocked eyes.

Seraphina put her hands on her hips and smirked. "I take it the two of you had no idea this was here."

"Not a clue," Seth said, and I shook my head. 'This' appeared to be a trap door of some kind. You almost couldn't tell it was there, even staring at it, the edges had been so well meshed with the other floorboards. I hurried forward, and Seth and Blair met us there, all of us kneeling beside it.

"You know, trap doors and hidden spaces typically mean secrets, and a lot of secrets are things you never wanted to reveal," Seraphina warned, looking straight into my eyes. "If I open this, whatever lies beneath is bound to change your life in some way."

Great. We were back to fate again, weren't we? It seemed I was right about destiny or fate or whatever the fuck you wanted to call it forcing us back to the manor house. "Just open the damn thing."

CHAPTER TWELVE

"Whoa, there, bud," Seth protested, putting his hand over it so Seraphina wouldn't lift it yet. "Maybe you should think it over before you get all hasty and shit."

I heaved a sigh. "I don't have time for you to play a fucking coward on me, Seth. The door's opening. I don't know what's in there. Maybe nothing. Or maybe, our parents, being secret angels and all, have something in there that could help us in case we don't make it to this portal in time. Now, kindly move your big fat hand and let's get on with it."

Seth moved but he wasn't at all happy about

it. Seraphina practically blew the door off, tossing it aside, and I stared down into a dark space. "Can't you, like, light it up or something?"

Seraphina scoffed. "I am air, not fire. If hot air could make a room glow, every room you step into would be on fire."

I couldn't be offended; it was too good of an insult. "Hold on, Dad," Blair said, and before I could stop him, he was out the front door. I cursed and would have run to the window to make sure nothing came for him in those few seconds, but he returned so quickly even my head spun. He held up two flashlights. "I'm going first," he said with a cocky grin.

"The hell you are!" Seth bellowed. "For all we know, there are demons down there that have broken out of their cages."

My son crossed his arms over his chest and glared at his uncle. "Maybe, but I'm not going to sit around like some scared little pansy. I want to know what's down there, and I'm going to go find out." At that moment, I was more proud of my boy than I ever had been.

"I'm right behind you, Blair," Seraphina told him, her eyes twinkling as she glanced at Seth. "How about that? A kid and a woman, both braver than the big, bad man."

I laughed so hard I couldn't help lower Blair into what looked like a bottomless pit from my angle, but as my son entered it with the flashlight, it proved to be only about twelve feet deep. Seraphina had him landing softly on his feet, and she floated down after him. I couldn't help thinking what a useful power that was and wishing I could do that shit.

I wanted to scream to Blair as he walked off out of view, but I held my tongue. I didn't want to seem overly concerned. Seth had already been razzed, and I wasn't going to stoop to his level. So, I waited. "Hey, Dad, Uncle Seth, you've got to see this!"

My brother and I exchanged looks, and I gave him a challenging smile. "I'll see you down below, coward." I leaped down, hearing Seth's mumbled curse, and I landed hard on concrete. The space had been carved out and reinforced long ago, it seemed, and as I gazed at the contents of the enormous underground room in the circles of Blair's flashlights, I felt like I'd stumbled into a treasure trove.

"What the hell is all this?" came Seth's voice as he finally joined us.

Blair panned over glass cases of what looked like ancient texts, artifacts, and weapons the likes of which I'd never seen. They were everywhere, lining the walls floor to ceiling, with the exception of the farthest wall from me, where a desk and chair covered in cobwebs were left. "I have no idea."

"Maybe this will help," Blair called, brushing the webs off the desk and uncovering a leather bound book. I marched over to him and yanked him back. "Dad, come on. It's a book. It's not going to bite my hand off."

"Just wait a minute. I don't want some ancient curse clinging to it to wash over you or anything." But as I stared down at it, with Seth hanging over my shoulder and Seraphina stepping up behind Blair, I knew it couldn't be cursed. The cover had been embossed with a gold-like substance that reminded me of the liquid gold and silver in the elemental's eyes, and I turned to look at her, wondering if she had anything to do with this. "Did you know what we'd find in here?"

She shook her head. "I did not know, but I suspected when I found it."

Of course she did. I turned back to the book, labeled *The Journals of Seamus McMullogh & The Legacy To Be Honored*. "Seth, did Dad tell you he kept journals?"

"No. Mom kept them, though." I turned as I heard paper rattle, and he held a similar bound volume. He showed me the cover, and written in a different hand, it said *The Diaries of Renee McMullogh, As Respects The Duty to the Heavens*. "What does that even mean?" he asked, his voice barely above a whisper.

Anxious, I reached for my father's book, turning to the first page. Aloud, I read, "As I enter into life on earth and renounce my life in heaven—"

"I endeavor to record all things my legacy must know in order that, should I pass before the time in which I bestow their heritage upon them, they have a written record to consult." I gaped at Seth as he finished the sentence, reading from my mother's journal. He looked up at me. "They had the same goal. They wrote the same thing, in case they died before they could explain all this shit to us."

Blair sat in the chair, throwing up a ton of dust and cobweb debris. "I'm not trying to be rude, but is there something else you haven't told me? Like, maybe it wasn't a plane crash that killed your parents?"

I leaned over him, flipping pages in Dad's journal and scanning without reading. "If it wasn't, then I'm clueless, too." And I was beginning to wonder. Had my parents had some sort of premonition of their death? Or was something already after them, even before I was born?

"There are those who can foresee the future,"

Seraphina interjected quietly. "Prophecies originally came from the divination bestowed by the heavens, but now, it is based on the visions of those who tap into evil. I would not hesitate to believe that the machinations to which you fell victim began longer ago than we at first realized."

"Maybe run that by me again in Prophecies for Dummies speak," Seth said, his face blank with confusion.

She pinched her face tightly. "Azazel has long been seeking a way to destroy those in the heavens in vengeance. I was aware of his manipulation of Amelia and her coven, but perhaps his plot did not start there." She motioned to the books Seth and I held. "In those writings, you might discover a reason Amelia chose you as opposed to another fallen angel. And in that discovery, it is entirely possible you'll find many of the circumstances of your life you considered to be random were, in fact, manufactured to create a specific result that brought you to Amelia. Desperation requires that one never leave anything to chance, and I assure you, Azazel is desperate."

The last thing I needed right now was reason to believe that a single entity had caused every tragedy in my life, from the death of my grandfather and parents to the betrayal of my ex-wife to the way I had to keep my son on the run from evil. I would gladly duel it out with the bastard until he was nothing but a puddle of rot on the ground.

My rage must have surfaced because I felt Seth's hand on my back, a calming touch he used when I was at my worst. "Simmer down, bro. I want a shot at this guy as bad as you do, but it sounds to me like that's already being covered with a much more epically painful fate for him than you or I could deliver."

It was true, but that didn't mean I wasn't thinking of at least 99 different ways to torture the instigator. "I'm fine," I growled, breathing deeply to try and bring down my blood pressure. "I think we should at least scan through these." I motioned to the two journals. They were obviously meant for us and contained all the things my parents had never gotten the chance to explain. Maybe we would find something of use in them, something that would allow us to stop running and face down our pursuers. *Save the boy, save the world.*

Yeah, it was corny, but it was accurate.

CHAPTER THIRTEEN

It was late when I finally pulled my head out of my father's journal. My hand suffered cramps from scribbling notes, and my eyes were going crossed from deciphering his very nice but incredibly slanted penmanship. Altogether, it made my head pound to consider the implications of the information I'd taken in, and I'd taken notes, knowing I couldn't quite process it all. Plus, I didn't know what my mother had felt was essential, so I had no idea if all of this was contained in the script Seth poured over.

All the while, Blair and Seraphina had

explored the other items in the basement hideaway, trying to figure out what each piece was and why it would have been hidden. The only interruption I'd had the whole time had occurred when Blair had picked up an innocent looking porcelain item that I would have guessed was some sort of telescope. Unfortunately, it turned out to be some sort of weapon that shot beams of light that singed the wall. They bounced around the room, making us all duck, until Seraphina managed to blow it into a corner and keep it there till it burned out.

A wide-eyed Blair had dropped it instantly, and Seraphina laughed. "Maybe you should let me pick things up to inspect them first. Many items in here are likely weapons that only activate at the touch of someone with angel blood."

I'd excused myself for a few minutes and used the ladder stowed down there to climb up and get some fresh air. Admittedly, I was a little freaked out at the time, and I'd nearly lost my cool. Seraphina had spiraled up to join me.

"Perhaps we should speak in the kitchen, or a room where your son is less likely to hear us."

I wasn't sure what she wanted, and I really didn't know if I was ready to hear it, but considering everything else, could it really be that bad? I grabbed one of the bags of chips we'd opened earlier and stress-ate while I waited to hear what glorious news she had for me.

"That weapon cannot be activated by a fallen angel. I've seen one like it only once before, and it can be used only by those still in the grace of the heavens." This was perhaps the first time I'd heard her frightened since first speaking about Amelia. "Blair should not have been able to activate it, with the mixed blood of a fallen angel and a witch. Something else resides in him."

I narrowed my eyes at her, not liking the sound of it. "What else would he be? You and Amelia have both told me that Seth and I are the children of two fallen angels. Are you taking that back now?"

Her brows drew together and formed a deep line in her otherwise perfect face. "I'm not sure what it means. All I can say is that I hope the answer lies in your readings."

Exasperated, I tossed the bag of chips on the counter and threw my hands in the air. "Don't you have a theory of some kind?"

"I have multiple theories, but I cannot equate any of them with what I just experienced," she threw back at me, her eyes sharp like a knife. I stared into them, falling into the liquid golden pools for a moment, and my gaze diverted only to find her full lips below. I wondered if they tasted as rich and sweet as they looked, and I wondered, if I was to try to kiss her, would she disintegrate into thin air to avoid my advances?

With my track record, I thought it best not to seek the answer to that question. Instead, I cleared my throat and stepped back to break the trance. "Fine," I responded in irritation, more at myself than her. "I guess I'll crawl back down into the dungeon and bury my nose in the fucking book again."

I stalked off and jumped into the basement, making Blair flinch as he caught sight of my face, which I knew was contorted into a disgruntled mask. I tried to give him a smile. "I'm not angry, son. You just scared the shit out of me."

Seth, barricaded behind some boxes, called out, "I think the boy scared the shit out of himself."

Blair looked down and toed his shoe at the floor. "I'll be more careful. I didn't know I could hurt someone."

I knelt in front of him, my heart melting. "It was an accident, and we all know that. None of us know much about the things in this room, and I didn't think it was dangerous, either. And really, if you don't explore, we'll never figure this damn place out."

He'd seemed relieved, and I'd gone back to reading.

Now, a few minutes before midnight, I found Blair dozing, sitting on the floor with his back against one concrete wall and his legs stretched out in front of him and Seraphina scanning through several documents she'd found in the file cabinet. As usual, she sat cross-legged in the middle of the room. Seth sat, looking dazed and rubbing his chin absently, either having finished our mother's journal or given up.

I didn't want to wake my son, and I turned to whisper to Seraphina. "Hey, can you do your handy little air thing and carry my son up to bed?"

She grinned broadly, setting the pile of papers on the floor and hopping to her feet. I watched in awe as Blair levitated into her arms, and she carried both of them out of the hovel. I scurried up the ladder to follow, but as I reached the ground floor, she twirled and disappeared, my son still in her arms.

I froze; if she'd been lying to us, she'd just won the battle because I'd been stupid enough to entrust her with my son's safety. I beat the hell out of myself for about ten seconds before she reappeared in a gust in front of me. "He's sleeping soundly in the southwest room upstairs. I tucked him in because it's a little drafty up there."

She would know, I supposed, and I slapped myself on the forehead for getting so worked up. I strode to the armchair my father used to sit in when he came to the library and flopped into it, running a tired hand through my hair. I needed to sleep, but my mind would never rest. I waited as Seth drug himself up out of the basement and sat with his legs dangling in the opening, looking about as alive as I felt.

"You two are sorry excuses for angels, you know," Seraphina teased. She looked at me. "You worry far too much. Look how well you've done so far, without really understanding your heritage. Now, you have access to every bit of that information, and you still feel inadequate." It struck a chord, but I didn't have time to analyze it too closely as she turned to Seth. "And you act like a blithering idiot, despite abnormal intelligence. Maybe if you spent as much time on useful information as you do on snarky comments, you'd have a little more self-confidence."

I snorted. I couldn't help it. We were all overtired, and her true but harsh comments were all the more hilarious because of it. "I guess I haven't done so bad, but Seth's been a big help."

"Yes, I have. Thank you," Seth said indignantly. He didn't take well to those sorts of comments.

Seraphina sighed. "I believe you should eat. Let's go to the dining room. I'll put together something edible, and we can discuss what you have found." Like lost puppies, we followed her without question. For me, the idea of food and the sway of her hips were enough to coax me along. I wasn't sure what motivated Seth, but he moved like a zombie, his eyes unfocused.

We waited quietly until our sudden caretaker arrived with tuna and canned vegetables wrapped in tortillas. It was fabulous. "By the time you finish those, I expect the shell-shocked expressions to disappear and the explanations to flow," Seraphina demanded. But as I looked up at her, she winked, and I could see the silver specks in her golden eyes again. I wondered if they stood out more in the throes of passion.

Seth must have been starving because his wrap disappeared, and the color returned to his face. Unfortunately, that also meant he found his voice. "Okay, Jax, I don't know what you got out of the million fucking pages you read, but I know the most important thing I read is that our mother wasn't a fallen angel."

I stopped moving, holding the wrap in front of me with my mouth open. Nothing in my father's texts had referenced her being anything else. I cast a sidelong glance at Seraphina, remembering our earlier conversation, and I slowly put down my food. She reached out and rested her hand on my arm, as if silently offering her strength, and I could have sworn my skin cooled and my muscles relaxed a minute degree.

Seth leaned on his elbows with an animated expression. He was ready for storytelling mode. "So, get this. Dad fell from the heavens after he met Mom, and she was devastated. They had secretly admired each other for a long time, and she saw her chance at happiness. So, she approached Hamied, the angel of miracles, and asked to be granted a mortal life on earth. Hamied told her she could live, not as a mortal, but as an angel. She would retain her powers in full but would not be granted access to the heavens." He smiled and spread his arms. "Our parents are, like, the ultimate fucking love story."

Seraphina squeezed my arm, and I smiled. "It sounds like Mom had a thing for bad boys."

"Yeah, that's what I don't get. She didn't mention why he was tossed on his ass into the bad neighborhood." Seth scowled as he gestured around us.

"Well, Dad did. It wasn't anything like Azazel's sin. He had a minor infraction." I hesitated, still not believing it myself. "He was a lower order of angel than Mom, and they'd arranged a meeting, sort of a date. Dad got anxious and crossed into the upper realm, and he got caught. When they asked him why he was there, he lied to keep Mom out of trouble. The lie cost him, and he was sent to earth."

Seth scoffed. "You obviously take after Dad. You're a fucking glutton for punishment, and you have the worst taste in women."

I was tired of hearing it, but I let it slide this time, mostly because the cool sensation Seraphina's hand sent through me suddenly shifted, and I started to feel warm all over, the heat starting at the point of contact. I shifted in my seat and, instead of getting pissed off, I tossed back, "Well, don't start comparing yourself to Mom, a hopeless romantic with a martyr complex. And you sure as hell aren't that pretty."

We probably would have gone on for hours, releasing our aggression in a healthy manner, but Seraphina cleared her throat, and we both turned our attention to her. Seth smirked. "Don't weigh in on this, cupcake. You and your little vanilla frosting on top. We all know whose side you'll take. Just so you know, this dumbass has never had a successful date in his life."

I don't know why that irritated me so much, but I was ready to give him an earful when Seraphina quipped, "That's quite a stone you're throwing from your glass house, considering I don't see a woman at your side." That effectively shut him up, and she finally released my arm and pressed her hands flat on the table. I felt so cold suddenly that I almost missed what she said. "I know why Azazel has grown so anxious."

CHAPTER FOURTEEN

"Well, by all means, share the knowledge," Seth invited, looking like a hungry wolf waiting for a rare steak.

Seraphina pulled her legs up under her in the chair, and I smiled. She was short enough her feet didn't touch the floor and dangled like a child's. I didn't know if it was uncomfortable or simply made her feel as if she couldn't be taken seriously. "To my knowledge, only twice before has an angel asked to be banished to earth, resulting in that angel retaining all heavenly powers. I doubt it would happen again in time to make arrangements prior to the Day of Judgment, which is near at hand."

I was at a loss. "Why does that make a difference?"

"Bear with me for a minute," she said, seeming to work things through in her own head as she spoke. "With your mother possessing her full powers and your father retaining some of his as a fallen angel, the two of you are more than just the spawn of fallen angels. You have the blood of a pure angel flowing through your veins." She looked up at me with a startled expression. "Do you understand now why Blair is so precious to this purpose?"

I felt like the answer was evading me, and I shrugged, taking the easy way out. Seth didn't seem to have a response, either. With a grave expression, the elemental explained, "I don't believe the blood of a fallen angel would be pure enough to fulfill the prophecy. However, a witch could never coerce an angel of full power to fall in love and have children."

She gazed at me apologetically, and I knew

why. "Well, at least I get a pass for being of a lesser order," I snorted. "Go on, you're not going to hurt my sensitive feelings."

"Well, that would make you the perfect target. That is, you or Seth. With the blood of an uncorrupted angel flowing through you, breeding with a witch provides a nearly perfect offspring. Your mother's heritage gives Blair additional power that likely lays dormant in both of you, and that blended with the blood of the witch is the ideal key." She pounded her fist on the table, and I jumped. "Under no circumstance can these witches get hold of Blair. They will never be able to reproduce the circumstances that led to his birth in time for Azazel to wreak his havoc."

As if I'd been slammed in the head by a wrecking ball, all the information suddenly shattered in my brain, but it was followed by the strange phenomenon of having them all fall into place. And as the picture became clear, my rage was devastatingly complete. I glared at Seth and seethed, "It all makes sense now. Mom and Dad didn't die randomly. They had to be removed before they explained our heritage and warned us against witches and other evils."

Seth nodded, and I could almost see the wheels turning behind his furrowed brow. "I'm sure Azazel had something to do with that. But think about it, bro. Their death also made us vulnerable in other ways, so that we were always looking to fit in, or to make some other poor bastard look stupid or weak." He pointed a finger straight at me. "If I hadn't been grandstanding, that loveless blue-eyed bitch would never have tunneled into your heart like a mole."

The more I thought about that, the more I understood every tragic event in my life. My parents *and* my grandfather had to die, any of them able to explain away the ghosts and the strength and all the things that made us different. And if my parents had survived, Seth and I wouldn't have been such menaces, getting in trouble and calling attention to ourselves.

But something else clicked, too, and I wanted to laugh as I turned to ask Seraphina, "Can angels, the pure ones, talk to the dead?"

"Well, I believe it's an important quality when greeting newcomers to heaven. How else would they communicate?" She said it as though it only made sense, and I couldn't believe how ridiculous I felt for not thinking of that sooner.

"Damn, that's a relief!" Her expression told me she thought I'd lost my mind. "I had horrible ideas about Blair. You know, I see them, Seth sees them, but Blair…he fucking hears them. And he talks back." I shook my head, chuckling. "I was so afraid there was something dark in him!"

Seth smiled, but it didn't reach his eyes, and I wondered about it until he changed the subject. "So, my nephew is some prophesied key, and likely the last hope for an evil, selfish son of a bitch who's had ages to marinate in his self-pity and agony while plotting his revenge. I gotta ask, Blondie, are you sure we're doing the right thing? Are you absolutely certain Blair can only open that gate one time?"

"Are you accusing me of lying? Or perhaps conspiring with the enemy?" I swallowed hard as her golden eyes flared, and I worried she would set fire to my brother in her indignation and offense. "I have been in the service of the heavens longer than you could fathom, and to betray my post would be a fate worse than death for me. I want nothing more than to stop the attack. Azazel has the power and can summon an army large enough to succeed. I will do whatever it takes to stop him from accessing the gates."

Seth stood and leaned over the table, narrowing his eyes at her. "Whatever it takes? Does that mean you would kill Blair before letting this bastard get to him?"

I nearly choked at the accusation. How had I not thought of that? The idea terrified me for a split second until I saw how Seraphina's face contorted. "If you question my loyalty to Blair, you know nothing about me. I would lay down my own life to save that child. I don't expect you to trust me, since you are the epitome of the skeptic and I've not yet proven myself. But you could kindly keep your negative opinion of me at bay."

I stood and put an arm around her shoulders, an automatic motion of comfort. As far as I was concerned, she had proven herself, and if there was any doubt left in my mind, her eruption just now removed it. She leaned into me for a brief second and then recovered as Seth stood, his eyes bugging out of his head, properly chastised.

"You know," I told her softly, "sometimes I have to just find the 'Seth' remote in my brain and hit the 'mute' button, just to maintain my sanity. You should probably do the same."

She looked up at me with a pout. "I don't have a 'Seth' remote. I can't mute it."

She was so serious and so morose in that moment all I could do was laugh, and we both turned to my brother in surprise when he joined in. He shook his head. "Damn, Finney, you are a crazy bitch, and I might regret it, but

I believe you."

She scowled at him. "Thank you. And do not call me Finney. I do not like that nickname at all." We laughed louder, only calming as Blair stumbled into the room, rubbing bleary eyes.

"What's going on, bud?" I asked, moving around the table to him and kneeling in front of him.

"Is something wrong? I heard yelling." His voice was hoarse with sleep, and I felt like an ass. Our bickering and revelry shouldn't have woken my son.

"No, Blair, we're just a bunch of raving lunatics who need to learn to shut our traps. Do you want me to take you back to bed?" Sure, he was twelve, but under the current circumstances, I think I would have wanted my father to carry me to bed and tuck me in at that age.

He nodded, and I grunted as I lifted him. He wasn't a baby anymore, that was for sure. As he laid his head on my shoulder, he yawned, "Can Seraphina come, too? She sings a really pretty song."

I couldn't answer for her, but she was beside me before I could turn to ask her. Together, we traipsed up the stairs, her light on her feet and me with my heavy load. I was strong, and I didn't tire easily, but carrying a person wasn't like lifting weights, and I was glad to discard him into the bed. He curled into a fetal position, and I draped the thick blanket over him as Seraphina sat on the edge of the bed and caressed his hair.

Her song had me transfixed, her voice like wind chimes and wooden flutes, the most beautiful tone I could ever remember hearing.

"Sleep in a peaceful place tonight
Never a worry or fear in sight
Let all your troubles drift away
Till the sun rises another day
Dream about fields of radiant beauty
Images of the bright sunlight
You will be safe in my embraces
Throughout the darkness of the night."

Blair was out like a light, and my heart

shattered. I gulped past the lump in my throat, and I turned on my heel, hurrying out of the room and down the stairs. I couldn't breathe, my lungs clenched tight in my chest, and I gulped at the cool air outside the manor house, staring out into the black night Seraphina had mentioned in her song.

Too many times I'd ached for my son. Too many times I'd imagined what it would have been like for him to have a mother who wasn't a liar, filled with hate. Too many times, I'd gone to bed, lonely and knowing I wasn't everything Blair needed. No matter how hard I tried, I couldn't replace his mother.

"What's wrong, Jax?" Seraphina's voice carried on the air like an echo from afar, but I knew she stood – or rather, existed – right behind me. I could feel the air swirl slightly, and my skin tingled the same way it had when she'd touched my arm before. "Why are you sad? Did I do something wrong?"

"Not at all." My voice was raspy with emotion, and I tried to clear it before speaking again. "You did everything right."

I felt her settle into the body she used next to me an instant before her fingers curled over my shoulder. "Then why are you sad?"

I turned to meet those gold eyes, not so brilliant in the darkness, except for the accented silver flecks, like stars in the sky. "I'm sad because Blair is twelve years old, and today is the first time anyone has sung him to sleep. I'm sad because my asinine mistakes mean he hasn't had a mother or even a mother figure. And you come in here like some glorious little fairy, whom I immediately attack because of my neurotic paranoia, and show him what he's been missing all this time." I scoffed. "Which is amazing, don't get me wrong. But when all of this is over, assuming we all make it out alive…" I sighed. "He didn't know what he was missing before, so he couldn't miss it."

"Jax, I have no intention of ever abandoning Blair," Seraphina told me. "When I swear myself to someone, I commit for life, and I have sworn to protect Blair." She smiled at me, a little shyly. "I am an energy and not exactly familiar with the emotion of love. But I believe that is what I feel toward Blair. I couldn't bear for anything to happen to him."

The words sank into my soul, and I nodded, blinking to keep tears from forming in my eyes. What was wrong with me lately? I was a big, strong guy, not some weeping, moaning idiot. "Thank you." I couldn't take my eyes off her, and I felt my body responding to her once again. I didn't just want to kiss her anymore; I *needed* to.

But I'd denied myself a great many things over the years for the greater good, and I could do it again. I forced myself to turn away, muttering, "I need to get some rest so we can start out early in the morning." I didn't look back as I strode through the house and upstairs to an empty room, ignoring Seth's snoring on the couch as I passed.

CHAPTER FIFTEEN

I probably shouldn't have taken the wheel, but I was grumpy and didn't want to sit in the passenger seat and wallow in my thoughts while wringing my hands all day. Unfortunately, Seth, too, was in a less than stellar mood, while Blair couldn't sit still. If I hadn't known better, I would have thought he'd had a couple of mugs of coffee, three or four candy bars, and maybe even some speed. I'd never quite seen him so amped, and I kept glancing in the rearview mirror at Seraphina, who sat calmly, save for singing along with Blair to the blasting radio and dancing in the seat now and then.

I couldn't seem to take my mind off her, even though my son should be my greatest concern. And he was; but we were prepared as best we could be and headed to thwart the best efforts of my ex-wife and her vengeful master. Even as I thought about it, I imagined some bad sorcery movie, with a big barbarian pulling sword from a stone, slaying a dragon, and rescuing a virgin about to be sacrificed in a filmy white dress.

And then, I pictured that dress on Seraphina, with rosy nipples visible through the thin material and her gold eyes and full lips worn in a mask of seduction.

I shifted in the seat, and my hand slipped, causing the Jeep to jerk a bit. I righted our path, but not before Seth caught on. "What the hell was that? Are you trying to pry your drawers out of your ass or what? You need to pull over for that shit. We're going far too fast for you to take a fucking chance like that."

Glancing back at Seraphina and Blair in hopes they weren't affected, I saw the hint of a smile on her face, while Blair didn't seem to care at all. "Sorry," I muttered.

But she wasn't about to let it go. "I seem to remember you spinning out as you tried to shake our tail yesterday, Road Warrior."

Seth smirked. "Well, you would be one to know about shaking tail, wouldn't you?"

Without missing a beat, she returned, "And you'd know about tucking yours in fear."

I chuckled, and I heard Blair's laughter floating in the air behind me. It was nice to see Seth warming up to our new ally, in his own way. The banter and wisecracks spoke volumes about his comfort level with her, and I was even proud of her for throwing back some really harsh comments.

The levity helped elevate my mood, and I began to sing along with the radio as well, which apparently irritated the hell out of my brother, who wore a perpetual scowl as we blasted our way back toward our route.

The time began to pass swiftly, and it seemed like no time at all before we had to stop for gas. "Dad, can't we stop and eat somewhere?" Blair complained. "I can't stand anymore canned food or gas station hot dogs. I've had my fill of veggies and grease."

I had, too, and seeing a diner up the street, I made an executive decision. I nodded toward it. "Why don't you all head up to the diner, and I'll meet you up there after I fill up?" We were in the middle of nowhere, a nothing town, and the diner was within my view. Plus, it wasn't like I was sending Blair without escorts. Between Seth and Seraphina, I felt certain he'd be safe. "Just don't run off, boy. Stay with Uncle Seth and Seraphina."

He nodded excitedly, and even Seth looked relieved at the thought of real food. I leaned against the side of the Jeep while it guzzled from the pump, watching the three of them, Blair walking backward and squinting in the bright sunlight as he smiled and talked to Seraphina and Seth staring off to the side, looking surly and discontent. I didn't know what had crawled up his ass, but I wanted to drill it out sooner than later.

Seraphina, on the other hand, captivated my attention, her hips swaying with each stride and her blond hair bouncing and reflecting rays of light that would likely blind an attacker. If Amelia had made my blood boil, this creature set my whole body on fire and melted the blood vessels within. Under other circumstances, I would have already made a move, despite my track record. But it was a lost cause now. Too many circumstances stood in the way, not the least of which was knowing that relationships forged under extreme or stressful situations never lasted.

The pump clicked, and I hung it up, twisting the gas cap on and closing the flap. I climbed back in the driver's seat and drove less than a block to park in front of the quaint little diner. It reminded me of the old couple who ran the diner back in our farce of a home, and I missed them. But I took a deep breath and realized that, if we could just take care of this business, we could go back; build a real home and a real life. That gave me strength and kept my mood from falling.

My traveling companions had taken a booth at the back and were scanning the menus. I stood in the doorway, smiling as Seraphina pointed out things to Blair, who seemed to think each thing looked better than the last. Yes, Bergina had been right; he could probably eat this place out of business if we stayed long enough. I made a mental note to order something to go so I could keep the boy's stomach from eating itself.

I strode over and sat next to Seth, who grunted as he scooted to make room for me and muttered, "Lard ass."

"Bubble butt," I returned, and I was rewarded with two sniggers across the table. "So, what looks good?"

"Everything," came the chorus of all three voices. As I grabbed a menu, I had to agree, and I thought perhaps we could all use a 'to-go' item for later down the road. As the waitress came over, chaos broke loose, everyone trying to order at once, and I held up a hand to call my little traveling band to order.

"Let's not be archaic here. Ladies first, then children." I smiled at Seth. "I would say age before beauty, but I take both categories, so I'll just go last."

As we ate our fill and ordered dessert, I reveled in the moment. This was how life should be, the way normal families functioned. Seraphina completed our little gang, taking a place I hadn't realized was empty. I wondered if Seth felt it and had to believe he did, since even his mood brightened with the opportunity to launch an assault of less than loving remarks at Seraphina. I didn't have to question the effect on Blair; I'd never known him to be this lighthearted.

I vowed that, if we managed to come out of this adventure alive and intact, I'd find a way to build something this complete. Blair needed a mother figure, and I needed someone to erase the bitter taste of a morbidly failed relationship. I wasn't sure Seth would ever find a woman willing to put up with his bullshit, but even he needed a warm body to cuddle at night. Maybe it would actually help him settle down a bit to fall in love.

CHAPTER SIXTEEN
AZAZEL'S DECLINE

"Azazel, favored son of the heavens, you were given immortality and unbound power, and you chose to betray your creator. Have you anything to say for yourself?" Raphael's voice thundered in the vast forum, bounced off the gold and pearl surfaces surrounding him, and Azazel shrunk at the painful throbbing it caused in his ears.

Battered and bruised from his capture in the human form he'd taken, he was weak, and weakness angered him. He knelt with his head bowed, but he did not offer penance. "You, like me, are made in the image of God, and as such, we should not be denied glory. Glory I found in the love of women. Glory I found in teaching them beauty. And glory I found in their gratitude for learning to wield magic. You, Raphael, choose to bow before an entity no stronger than you and I will never experience the glory of true love, or of passion, and you will leave behind no legacy of family." He raised his head and snarled at the beast who would sentence him unfairly for what should never have been considered a transgression. "Given the choice, I would gladly renounce my place in heaven for such a beautiful experience."

Azazel cried out as the golden whip lashed across his back, splitting flesh almost to the bone, and he felt the rivulets of blood trickling down his spine. He ground his teeth and clenched his fists, wishing he could transform and fight the angel before him fairly, for Raphael would lose. Azazel was the stronger of the two, and more charismatic than any of those still in God's graces.

He sought fulfillment, completion he could not find in the heavens, and for his determination, for filling a void within his soul, he would be banished, and likely tossed into the fires of hell to writhe in pain for all eternity. A fair god, so many believed. But Azazel knew otherwise. The god worshiped by humans was not fair, was not forgiving. Once a faithful servant, Azazel no longer believed his creator loved him but rather used the angels to accomplish his handiwork without reward. He believed God had created man for amusement, toyed with them needlessly, and exacted punishment on those both in heaven and on earth who dared question his authority.

Raphael stepped down from the platform and approached Azazel, a sinister look in his glowing eyes that should never reside on the face of a heavenly creature. "You sought glory and destroyed human relationships with God. You corrupted entire nations with desires of the flesh and of worldly things. You, Azazel, former subject of God, are banished from the heavens. For the enormity of your sins, you will no longer reside on earth to wreak havoc on the faithful and true. I banish you to a pit of darkness."

Azazel stared in stunned silence at his prosecutor, judge, and jury. A searing pain around his wrists and ankles made him gasp, and his body contorted, his arms drawing behind his back and his ankles crossing. "You are to be bound, hand and foot, by the rope of flame, and you will lie on a bed of jagged rocks beneath the desert, never to see the sun or feel the cool breeze, never to rest in comfort." Raphael took one more step and threw out his hand.

The sensation of falling overwhelmed Azazel's poor human body, and he faded in and out of consciousness as he sank deeper and deeper below the surface of the earth, Raphael's voice still ringing in his ears. "Your face shall be covered so you may only scent the foul stench of your own lying snake's tongue and may not consider your own reflection in narcissistic love. Be gone, Azazel, and know that the day you surface from the eternal tomb in which you are buried alive will be the Day of Judgment, when you and your kind are cast into the fires of hell. You will cease to exist."

Forever, Azazel continued to fall until he lost all sense of time and space, of gravity and of existence. At long last, he landed, and the jagged rocks stabbed into his back, scraping and cutting and gouging as he screamed for release. The utter darkness was terrifying, even to an angel of his former stature.

For countless days and years and centuries, he lay there, silently cursing those who had betrayed him, but most of all hating Raphael, who could have destroyed him but had chosen a torment worse than anything the rebellious angel Lucifer could ever have imagined. And in the moments he felt he could no longer keep his sanity, or survive the pain and loneliness, he imagined the sweet revenge he wanted to exact on the heavens.

When his spirit arose from his body, he thought he had finally died, and it confused him, knowing that Raphael had purposely left his immortality intact so he would suffer eternally. And as he looked around, finding he was nothing more than an apparition, he gazed into the most beautiful of blue eyes. Before him stood a woman, an infant in her clutches, and her smile told him all he needed to know about her intentions.

"I have something for you," she said, her voice like the smoothest wine. He'd thought she meant the child, but instead, she'd opened a scroll, ancient and written in a very old language even he could barely read. "This is the Scroll of Power. If you decipher for me how to become all-powerful, I and my coven, for all of eternity, shall bow to you and do your bidding, with you, Azazel, as the sole creature deemed greater than we are."

As he'd read the scroll, a plot had formed, and he saw hope for the first time. Gazing at the tiny child, little more than a few days old, he told the witch, "Give me her name."

Holding the child up for him to see fully, she said, "This is my daughter, Amelia."

CHAPTER SEVENTEEN

Worriedly, I stormed up to Blair's room early in the morning. He never slept in and was usually dressed and eating before I could peel my eyelids open. But as I opened the door to the room that had once been mine, I found him still out cold, only his fiery crown visible above the blankets.

I hated waking him, but it was time to get back on the road, and I wasn't in the best of moods, having slept poorly myself. I clenched my jaw and went looking for Seth to have him do the deed, but he was MIA, which only irritated me more. I ran into Seraphina first, literally, as I rounded the corner into the kitchen and she came bustling out.

"Sorry," I grumbled, reaching to help her balance the load of food she carried, but she already had everything settled on the little air pockets she could create, nullifying any use I could be.

"It's alright," she told me brightly. "Are you alright?"

I ran my fingers through my hair impatiently. "I'm fine, just tired. I can't find Seth, and my son has decided today is the one day of his entire childhood he's going to sleep in."

She touched my arm, and it should have been soothing. Instead, it was like a match to lighter fluid, and my veins exploded with fire. "Seth is out front on the phone. If you want, I'll go rouse Blair while you seek him out."

I was grateful but couldn't seem to form the words. Instead, I frowned at her magically balanced load. "What's all this?"

"I thought we might want some food for the

road. Stopping obviously wasn't of much help yesterday, and I think it best we try to minimize breaks." Her eyes were wide, as if she felt like I was chiding her for doing something wrong.

I scrubbed my face with both hands. "Thank you, it's a great idea. I wish I'd thought of it, and I'm glad Seth didn't." I gazed toward the front door. "Are you sure you're okay with waking up a twelve-year-old who's likely in the middle of a dream?"

"I think I can handle it." She took off upstairs, food floating around her like satellites, and a part of me wanted to be in her orbit, too. The other side of me knew I shouldn't let her get any closer to Blair. Of course, talking to Seraphina last night had cleared my concerns a bit, but it hadn't eased my conscience. I didn't know why I couldn't reconcile my feelings regarding their relationship, and I wondered if it was my own loneliness, maybe leading to irrational fear that they would form a parental bond and leave me alone with my brother.

I threw open the front door and stared at Seth as he paced in front of the house. He held up a finger to stop me from talking, and I crossed my arms and waited. When he finally hung up, I lashed out, "Are you ready to go? Or are you wasting time calling a fucking stock broker to make money we'll never spend if we don't get on the road?"

To his credit, Seth didn't spew a retort. "Actually, I was explaining why we missed our flight last night to the wonderful travel agent who kindly got us a partial refund. And that was after calling the maid to explain to her that we'd allowed a couple of friends to crash here last night so she wouldn't have a fucking meltdown, thinking there were ghosts here."

I opened my mouth to remind him that, at least in the past, there were, but he winced, realizing exactly what I was thinking, and that was good enough for me. "We're leaving in twenty minutes," I told him, turning back toward the door.

"What the hell crawled up your ass last night, bro?" Seth called, and I froze. "Your attitude sucks."

"Yeah, so do you," I called back and slammed the door behind me, heading to the basement space to see if there was anything in it that might come in handy on our trip.

***

Blair was bleary eyed and rested his head on Seraphina's arm as I drove away from the house full of memories, old and new. I was still reeling from what we'd found and what we'd read, but most of all, I was starting to obsess over my son's confidence in the most recent addition to our band of brothers. At some point, I would have to come to terms with the fact that my son needed her strangely nurturing ways and that, perhaps, so did I. But today was not going to be that day. After all, the circumstances were dire, and it made me tense.

I glanced at Seth, who stared out the passenger window pensively as we drove through the barren outskirts of several Arizona towns. I'd taken the highway less traveled, refusing to get us into the shit storm of off-roading we'd tried once before while still hoping to avoid a tail. We couldn't risk the wasted time. If Amelia and her coven figured out where we were headed, we were screwed three ways to Sunday.

Seth rarely retreated into his head as he had now, and I realized our discoveries had affected him as much as me. I tended to be a little selfish at times, forgetting that I wasn't the only one in a mess of trouble, and it wasn't fair. Seth had been my constant support system in protecting my son, a loyal brother to the end.

Unfortunately, I didn't feel like discussing anything, especially with Blair passed out behind us and Seraphina wide awake and alert. Our family business was our business, no matter how much of a help the air elemental had been, and I didn't want to give her anymore insight to us than she already had. And I certainly didn't want to wake my incredibly tired son.

The miles rolled by, and time seemed to float

away. I felt like a drone on autopilot, my mind going blank except for the determination to get to our destination safely and ahead of the enemy. I wasn't drawn out of my 'nothing box' until Seth leaned over and gazed at the dash meaningfully. "I think we should stop for gas in the next town."

I looked at the gauge and cursed. "How the fuck did that happen?" We hadn't gotten nearly as far as I'd thought we would on the gas we had. Then again, I had forgotten we weren't on a full tank when we left the house. With a sigh, I told him, "We're about twenty miles out of Snowflake. I wanted to get into New Mexico before we stopped, but we'll get gas there."

Seth nodded. "Are we ever getting on 40? It's the fastest way across."

I shook my head. "It's too obvious a route. When we stop, I need your trusty map skills to find us another way that's less noticeable and doesn't lose a lot of time. And don't even think about forging our own road."

He gave me an offended look. "You act like we nearly died or blew a tire the first time. You're a fucking drama queen."

"Just do what I ask, okay?" I had a bad feeling about getting off the road. We were making good time, and there had been no strange sensations of being followed or watched. For some reason, I had the impression that, if we kept going, it would stay that way, but if we stopped, I expected the worst. I wasn't one to have premonitions, so I tried to let it go, but the disconcerted feeling got worse as I pulled into a mom and pop gas station on the outskirts of an already small town.

I pulled out cash and sent Seth to pay, and Blair yawned and stretched, finally coming to life. I pointed to him. "Stay there until I can come with you to the bathroom. We're in and out in less than thirty seconds, got it?"

He scowled at me. "There's that paranoia again," he grouched. He looked up at Seraphina, whose face was a mask of stoicism, and I wondered what she was thinking or if she sensed something.

She tapped her fingers on her chin. "It's just to be safe, Blair. Your father's right. We can't be too careful now." She turned to me. "I'm going to scout the area."

I nodded, narrowing my eyes and knowing she didn't feel comfortable about our location. "Like you said, we can't be too careful," I commented. She blew away in her whirlwind, and I guessed she probably had a better grasp on anything out of the ordinary as little more than a breath of air. For some reason, I imagined I could still smell her, and I grunted at myself for even noticing.

Focusing back on my job, I barely turned to look at the gas pump as I set up to fill the tank, not wanting to let Blair out of my sight.

CHAPTER EIGHTEEN
BLAIR'S ESCAPE

"You're not coming in the bathroom with me, Dad." I was dead set, and Dad's irritated look didn't make me change my mind. "You can wait right outside the door for me, okay? And I'll go right to Uncle Seth when I get out so you can take a leak."

He was reluctant, but he nodded. "Fine. Hurry up." He was being so overprotective I wanted to scream, but a part of me understood his worry. Now that I knew what was going on, I was a little scared, too, but I wasn't going to let him know that. He'd start treating me like a five year old again, and I didn't want that.

Besides, as I stepped into the bathroom and locked the door to make sure he wouldn't try to follow me after all, I could feel Seraphina's energy in the air outside, and it made me feel safe. I did my business, washed my hands, and looked at my reflection for a second. I didn't look like anything special, although I had always been a little freaked out by my own eyes. I was the only kid I knew with two different colored eyes, and I wondered if that was a sign that I was special.

Dad knocked on the door impatiently. "Are you alright?"

I rolled my eyes and yanked the door open. "I'm fine, Dad. It would be nice if I could empty my bladder in peace, though."

He pointed to Uncle Seth, standing next to the Jeep and looking like he needed to piss worse than any of us. "Straight to the Jeep. I want you buckled in when I get there."

I gave him a sarcastic salute as he went into

the bathroom, and I started toward my uncle. I felt a strange sensation, like a quick blur of my vision, an instant before I was yanked backward. I grunted, and I kicked, but my feet didn't touch anything. I started to panic, but a beautiful voice sounded in my head. *Don't be afraid, no one is going to hurt you.*

I wasn't sure I believed that, but my body relaxed anyway, and as I looked around, suddenly unable to move at all, the desert passed by at least three times as fast as it did when Uncle Seth floored the Jeep. Then, the sand and dirt were gone, and I flew through trees and up the side of a mountain.

I stopped and thumped on my butt on the ground. My arms and legs and neck were working again, and I looked all around me, getting into a crouched position and ready to run or defend myself if necessary. Dad was going to freak the hell out when I was gone, and I was going to do everything I could to make him proud of me when I got out of this mess.

I tried to remember what Uncle Seth had

taught me about details. *Know all the details, wherever you are, or if you try to escape, you won't get very far.* I noticed first the campfire, blazing bright and much too close to the trees for camping safety. There were also several tents set up randomly and not very well. Some of them looked like a breeze would knock them down.

Whoever was here, they were better at kidnapping than camping.

The trees weren't thick or tall, but I imagined it was hard to find a real forest somewhere like Arizona. I had a pretty good idea who had taken me, and as a thin woman with blue eyes the color of one of mine slipped out of one of the tents and came toward me, my suspicions were confirmed.

I'd always wanted to see a real witch.

This one wore a long, white dress that hugged her body like a cloth and draped on her arms and around her legs. Her hair was dark brown, almost black, and her skin had a dark, olive tint. She was a total babe, and my mouth gaped a little as she stopped a few feet in front of me, dropped to her knee, and bowed.

"Good morning, my liege," she said, and I recognized the voice as the one from my head earlier. She lifted her face to me, and I noticed a pendant at her neck, but I couldn't tell what it was. "I am honored to have you at my encampment."

Feeling tough, I smirked. "I would think so, since you need someone like me to fix up the tents before they collapse. A drop of rain could bring those down around you the way they're set up."

I'd been going for tough and offensive. Instead, she smiled, and her eyes glowed with something like interest or maybe gratitude. Apparently, Dad was right about one thing. Witches were crazy bitches.

"Your kind offer is appreciated. However, we won't be staying much longer." She stood, and I averted my eyes. I didn't want to look at her body. It was messed up to find someone evil attractive, wasn't it? Especially someone who was probably old and glamoured and looked like an old hag underneath.

I glared at her. Maybe they weren't going to stick around, but I wasn't leaving unless it was to go back to Dad, Uncle Seth, and Seraphina. "If you're so glad to meet me, the least you could do is tell me who the hell you are."

She pushed her lips together in a thin line, and she already looked older. "I see your father hasn't raised you with appropriate manners. You should watch your language, young man."

I laughed like her presence didn't terrify me. "So, first, you bow down and call me your 'liege', and now, you're lecturing me on respecting my elders. I think you're a little mixed up, lady. And for the record, since you yanked me here without my permission and haven't even introduced yourself, I don't owe you any respect."

Her eyes turned stormy, and I swallowed the cry of fear that came up my throat. I wasn't going to let her scare me, and I wasn't going to act like a kid. Almost as fast as she'd become angry, she slipped back into the sweet, grateful personality she wore like a costume. "I apologize for my lack of courtesy."

I waited, but she didn't say anything until more women started crawling out of the tents, and in less than a minute, I was surrounded by at least two dozen witches, maybe more. They were all different shapes, sizes, ages, colors, but they wore similar clothing, and they all had the blue eyes that I'd obviously inherited from the more screwed up side of my family.

The witch who stood in front of me, in the middle of the circle watching, held out her arms like she was gesturing to the rest of the witches and the forest all at once. "Welcome to the Estelle Coven. I would have liked to introduce you to our home, but that's not an option at this time." She lowered her arms, and gave me a smile that wasn't exactly pleasant. "I'm Amelia, and I've waited for this moment for a very long time, my son."

My mother.

I gulped, trying to decide whether to be terrified, angry, hurt or something else entirely. How was I supposed to feel about meeting my mother for the first time, considering she only had me to use me? She'd just kidnapped me, and now she was acting like I was an honored guest. From Dad's story, I didn't think she'd ever loved me, and yet, she acted like she wanted me here. She hadn't even mentioned what she wanted to use me for, and I didn't see any sign of an evil, power-hungry angel.

But how would I know what that looked like?

I tried to stick with the surly, teenage angst my dad always grouched about. "I hope you don't expect me to call you Mom and come running for a hug."

She laughed, and it was like music. It didn't sound evil. Either Dad was completely off his rocker, or she was a really good liar. "Well, maybe not today. I think, in time, you'll come to understand and love me." She came forward and crouched in front of me. I kept my guard up and prepared to react. "We have some work to do, young man, and I think I owe you an explanation."

I scoffed. "Dad pretty much gave me the rundown already. You set him up and made him fall in love with you, and then you got pregnant with me even though you said you didn't want kids yet. You had me because you and your weird ass family here are serving an evil angel who tried to ruin the earth, and now, you want to use me to open the gates to Heaven so the guy can kill off all the good angels who punished him. Does that cover it?"

She frowned, all the way to her eyes. "That's such a twisted tale, Blair. That's not how things are at all." She held out a hand to me. "Come, let's sit by the fire, and I'll tell you the truth."

I hesitated. I didn't want my head filled with bullshit, and I didn't know if witches could use mind control or brainwashing. But if I agreed to sit with her and I got her to talk, it would delay them from trying to carry me away from the people who would be frantically looking for me. I didn't have much hope of escape alone with this many insane women around, but I trusted my real family to come get me.

I didn't take her hand, but I stood and walked toward the fire by her, keeping a distance between us. I sat down and looked at her expectantly. "Well, let's hear it."

She was definitely a smooth talker, I thought as she began her version of the story. Honestly, it was like the Tim Burton version of a fairy tale, and I had to fight not to laugh at her. "Azazel was falsely accused of a great many things, and when Raphael passed judgment, he failed to gain the approval of the most high. It is duty to achieve justice, Blair. I'm sure your father and your uncle have taught you that."

I didn't like her using the lessons I'd learned to reel me in, and I didn't respond. She continued, "He wants to plead his case appropriately, to be absolved, before the Day of Judgment comes and he is erased unfairly from existence. It's like putting an innocent man on death row, my son."

I scowled at her. "My name is Blair."

She smiled as if she was just humoring a stupid kid, and no matter how sweet and charming she acted, I still didn't like her. "The only way to get him back to Heaven to speak to the true judge is with a key, and I agreed to provide that key. I wanted a husband, and I wanted a son. I chose your father, not because he was a fallen angel, but because he was the first fallen angel I'd met who made me feel whole. Whatever he's told you about me, I loved him very much, and I wanted you as my own. He stole you and disappeared the hour you were born, and I mourned for you, Blair."

I couldn't make sense of it. "Couldn't you have followed him? Or one of these other creepy women who won't give us any privacy?"

"They are watching for trouble, Blair. And your father has powers that shield your energy. We weren't able to track you. I was weakened from giving birth, and Jax took advantage of that. He was wrong, Blair. He never gave me a chance to be a mother to you, and because he's jealous, he's been running ever since."

What was she talking about? "What do you mean, jealous?"

A small line appeared between perfectly arched brows. "Dear boy, have you not noticed how your father feels about you getting close to that elemental now traveling with your group? Did he not speak poorly of her from the start? Does he not act as though she is untrustworthy?" I considered that, and she added, "Has that woman done anything to make you doubt her loyalty to you?"

No, she hadn't. Was Amelia – I couldn't think of her as my mother – saying that my father couldn't stand the idea of me being close to a woman I trusted? It would explain a lot, including the fact that he'd arranged for a bad date, probably hoping I wouldn't be interested in dating again for a very long time. And he still seemed to dislike Seraphina. I'd seen a couple of times when he looked in the rearview mirror at us, and he seemed so angry.

But why would he feel that way? Because he'd had poor luck with women? That was his fault for having such bad taste, as Uncle Seth always told him. But since Dad never took responsibility for any big mistake, he probably was jealous of the fact that Seraphina wanted to spend time with me and not him. Was that why he'd taken me from my mother?

"Listen, Blair, regardless of your father's disposition, we have work to do." She interrupted my thoughts. "Azazel had great rewards for us once we've helped him with his plight, and I'm sure the most high will lavish us with praise and rewards. Can you imagine being in the favor of god and the angels in such a way?" She clapped her hands like the girls at school who thought they were too cute. "And you, Blair, deserve such an elevated position most of all. You are too pure a being to settle for less."

I didn't want rewards. I just wanted to do the right thing. There were always two sides to a story, and even though I didn't believe my mother's version at all, I wondered if there was any truth to it at all. "How did you find out about Azazel? I mean, did he tell you all this? Because I thought he was trapped underground somewhere."

She gave me one of those long suffering smiles teachers got when they thought things like, *it's so cute how naïve he is.* "Sweetheart, not everything is literal. Besides, we all have some special powers. Azazel is an angel, and while he was stripped of his rights to Heaven, he's still incredibly powerful. As long as he lives, I doubt there will be a power that can keep anything more than his body imprisoned anywhere. With the combined power of this coven, we can give him some relief from his suffering."

That didn't sound like a positive thing, in my book, and I was the kid who talked to ghosts. I could only imagine what a normal person would think about that. Besides, I could think of a lot of other possibilities, including the fact that they could have summoned some demon who claimed to be Azazel. How would they know the difference? Did anyone know what this angel looked like?

Knowing I could play the innocent kid card, I asked, "How do you know he's not going to use you? If he has all this power, he could just use us to get into Heaven and then destroy all of us."

Several of the witches around us laughed, like I was stupid. That was fine; they would learn. I thought about Dad's story and how Uncle Seth had thought a little too much of himself with the football team. I wasn't going to try to beat the shit out of them, but I had full confidence I could outsmart them.

My mother shook her head. "We work together, Blair. Perhaps your father has taught you about betrayal rather than loyalty. I trust those with whom I work. Of course, this all goes back to the elemental traveling with you. She is a friend, right? And yet, once again, your father does not trust her."

Dad didn't trust anyone unless he could run background checks through at least three different agencies. Why did she keep coming back to Dad and Seraphina? Was there something going on with them I didn't know about? I suddenly understood Dad's paranoia. It was far too difficult to figure out who you could trust.

"Leave them out of this," I told her. "You wanted me, and now you've got me. What are you going to do with me?"

She smiled; one of those sweet, sugary smiles old women get that gives you chills. "I need your help, Blair. We're going to open the gates to Heaven so Azazel can confront Raphael and seek out true justice from the entity who should have made the decision the first time."

Dad and Uncle Seth and Seraphina had planned to do the same thing. They were taking me to open the gates because, apparently, I was a 'disposable' key and could only be used once. I would open the gates and then close them, which meant my mother, her coven, Azazel, and anyone else who wanted to get in were shit out of luck. If I couldn't get away from these looney tunes, I could always stick to that plan. I wasn't sure my mother was lying, particularly, but I was sure that anyone banned from Heaven likely deserved it, and I wasn't about to let this guy go in with guns blazing.

I nodded. "Okay, how do we do it?"

She seemed pleased. "We have to get to a portal that allows us to move between the realms. Then, you simply open the door. See? It's not even a hard job."

My mind raced as I formed a plan, the likes of which would make Dad and Uncle Seth jealous of my mental capabilities. I screwed my face into a frown of concentration, needing to keep up the act, and told her, "I heard something about a portal. I think they said it was in New Orleans."

Several of the witches muttered to each other, and now, my mother's face was all business. "Then we shall go to New Orleans." She put a hand on my shoulder, and I felt slimy, like some sort of evil goop dripped from her fingertips down my arm. But I didn't pull away. I was supposed to be on her side now. "You'll be happier than you can imagine when this is done, I promise."

If everything went the way I planned, there were two outcomes. Either I would be as happy as she said, no longer on the run, or I would be dead. It was scary, and part of me was angry that I had to carry a weight like this. I didn't ask to be a key. But part of me was excited at the adventure, and I couldn't wait to finally be part of the action.

CHAPTER NINETEEN

"Why the fuck weren't you watching him?" I exploded at Seth, sweating profusely after searching the entire area for at least a thousand foot radius. "I sent him to you!"

Seth raged back. "He was with you, dumbass! You sent me to pay for the gas, and when I got back, you took off for the head. You didn't say jack shit about watching for the kid to come back, and I sure as hell didn't expect you to let him out of your sight! Why would you blame this on me?"

I wasn't blaming anyone in particular. Or maybe I was deflecting because it was my fucking fault my son had disappeared without a trace in a matter of seconds, and I didn't want to accept responsibility. On top of that, I was out of my mind with dread like I'd never felt about anything in my entire life. Blair knew better than to run off. He knew everything about our situation now, and I couldn't believe he would purposely do something to scare the shit out of me.

That meant my worst nightmare had come true. Only one entity could have slipped in and out that quickly, without detection, and I knew I'd been kidding myself to think that Amelia wasn't on our tail the whole time. She'd always been a master manipulator and an opportunist. That's how we'd met, wasn't it? She'd taken advantage of an opportunity to grab my undivided attention.

I felt the brisk wind that told me Seraphina had joined us again, and the guilt of blaming her at first overwhelmed me. She'd been an easy target, since she was the infiltrator in our group and had conveniently not been visible when Blair was taken. But then, she'd shown up, frantic at having sensed Amelia's presence and, because of some shield the witches had erected, Seraphina had been unable to materialize.

She'd helped us search and, at one point, she'd told me she was going for help. I didn't know what sort of help she meant, but I would take anything I could get at that point.

She materialized beside me, looking harried, and before I could demand to know where she'd been for the last half hour, I felt a blast of radiant heat at my back, like something had exploded behind me, and I turned to catch the last of the flame as it died, revealing a devilish looking creature, tall and gaunt with black eyes rimmed in red and a very angular chin. His hair was black and long, pulled back into a braid tied with a leather strap, similar to the style of some Native Americans, and his bare chest above his jeans made me feel a little insecure in my own masculinity. I definitely needed to tone up a bit.

"Who the fuck are you?" Seth asked, staring at him with wide eyes.

Seraphina stepped forward. "This is Shila. He's a fire elemental, and he's agreed to help us."

I failed to see what this stranger, who looked more like every image of the devil I'd seen than the same type of magical being Seraphina was, could do for us. "I'm sorry, I don't mean to be rude. But there's not a trace of Blair anywhere, and I don't understand what this guy can do for us."

Shila gave a curt nod. "I get that a lot. I am a fire elemental, and I can track anything. I will seek out the trail they are likely not even aware they left, and I will find where they have taken your son."

I stared at him, feeling Seth tense behind me, and I knew he didn't trust the guy. But I trusted Seraphina, probably far more than I should have, and if she had gone to this creepy man for help, I trusted him as well. "Where do we start?"

"You cannot follow me." His words were flat, and I heard Seth's incredulous scoff. I kicked at his shin, and he cursed, but I wanted to hear the rest of what Shila had to say. "My tracking is not done in a physical form. Seraphina will come with me, and she will return to take you to your son and his captors."

"Am I supposed to sit here and wait? Not do anything for however long it takes?" I wasn't ungrateful, I just wasn't sure I could survive that kind of torment, the not knowing and not being able to take any action.

Seraphina put her hands on my cheeks, drawing my attention, and I looked down into calm, reassuring eyes. "Time does not pass for us as it does for you. We can find Blair and be back in a matter of minutes, or even less." Those golden orbs were hypnotizing, and the longer I looked into them, the more I wanted to kiss her pouty lips. "We'll find him, Jax. You have my word."

The heat of her touch seemed to relax me, and that calm surged through my body until I nodded in response. "I'll be right here," I told her, my voice hoarse with emotion.

She pushed up on her toes and kissed my cheek. I closed my eyes and held my breath, praying like hell it wasn't too late, and opened them to a swirl of fire, wind, and dust as the two elementals took off on their hunt.

"What the fuck are you thinking, Jax?" Seth railed at him, shoving my shoulder. "You know, that bitch could've been in on this the whole time, and now, she's got backup. They're gone, and they've got Blair!"

I whirled, my anger and terror spilling out on him. "Can you just shut your goddamn mouth for two minutes, Seth? I didn't have a choice here. We've got nothing else to go on! And I don't want to hear another word about Seraphina betraying us. Do you know how many times she could have made off with Blair by now? Hell, she could have run off with him when you tied her up. But she's been here with us, helping us."

"Oh, please, Jax, are we really going to have this conversation right now? Once again, your taste in women fails you, and you need to start thinking with the head on your shoulders and not the one in your pants."

I didn't think; I launched a punch square at his jaw, and his head snapped to the side. The force nearly knocked him down, and I braced for his reaction. But he righted himself, giving me a glare that should, by all rights, have burned me to the ground and pointed at me with one hand as he held his jaw with the other. "One pass, dear brother. That's all you get is one."

I watched him pop his jaw, my fists clenching and unclenching at my side, and the bruise was already forming low on his cheek. He shook his head. "You are a son of a bitch, Jax, and you're damned lucky I love you like I do. I probably should have kept my mouth shut, so I'll let this go, but you seriously need to get your shit under control."

Never, in all my life, had I lashed out at Seth like that, and I was already starting to regret it. I just didn't know what to do with myself. I was shocked no one had showed up to try and take us down, and it worried me. Were they that confident in their ability to hide Blair, or had they used him and killed him already?

I sat on the bumper of the Jeep, my head in my hands, and fought the urge to scream or cry or laugh hysterically. Any of those options were weak, and I wasn't weak. I had all these powers, didn't I? How was it possible they were useless?

Then again, maybe they weren't. If I could sense bad juju around me, why couldn't I sense my son's good energy? I reached inside for that sonar and concentrated as hard as I could. Even if I couldn't find Blair, maybe I could *feel* him, at least enough to know he was alive and well. I pictured his red hair, his mismatched eyes rolling at a bad joke I told, and I called up the sound of his laughter. It all came together, and I reached out for the feeling it called to mind, seeking it as an active force somewhere in the universe.

"What are you doing now?" Seth's voice threw me out of my trance, and I could have punched him all over again. I shot to my feet, ready for the brawl I'd been hoping for, only to be blasted with a gale force wind once again, my face burning with the explosive heat of Shila's return.

"Your son is with the coven, in Gila National Forest," Shila said.

Seth was already on the map, tracing a route. I breathed a sigh of relief, ready to collapse at the news. "So he's alive."

"He has not been harmed."

"Thank you, Shila," Seraphina told him, exchanging a strangely intimate look with him that almost made me want to crack the guy's jaw, my stress at the breaking point and a surge of jealousy throwing me over the edge. "I appreciate your help."

"It was a favor owed, and I keep my promises. Good luck to you, old friend. May your journey not be burdensome, and may your toils be rewarded." With that strange bidding, he burst into flames and left behind a few ashes blowing around on the ground, like some damn phoenix ready to be reborn.

Seth made for the driver's seat, but Seraphina

beat him to it. As he prepared to protest, she told him, "It would be easier if I didn't have to shout directions from the backseat. Besides, I know how far out we need to stop to avoid being detected and thwarted."

I was glad someone had a plan, since I was at a loss. Seth glanced at me as I climbed into the passenger seat and grumbled as he hopped in the back. I caught something about women and the last time he'd been shoved in the back because of a woman ending badly, but I didn't get to tell him to shut his trap as Seraphina floored it. I instantly had a terrifying thought and shouted over the wind, "Do elementals spend a lot of time behind the wheel?"

"Not really," she responded, not taking her eyes off the road. "But watching from afar gives some of us a really good idea of how it's done." Her words didn't inspire confidence, and I reached for my seat belt, seeing Seth doing the same with a deathly pale complexion. "I promise we'll be fine."

I wasn't sure she could keep that promise as the needle crept toward the far right of the speedometer, especially as she jerked the wheel, veering off the road toward the south. I white-knuckled the roll-bar, expecting to fly out at any time, but as we sped over the rocky, cracked terrain, the bouncing eased, and I couldn't believe how gently the Jeep was riding at such high speed for off-roading.

It took a moment, but I realized Seraphina had us on a pocket of air that kept the car from hitting the rough spots along the way, and I marveled at just how useful her talents were. Why couldn't mine be so valuable when it came to rescuing my son?

CHAPTER TWENTY
BLAIR'S RESCUE

One of the older witches offered me some food, and my stomach growled, but I didn't trust it. I had images of throwing up my feet or being controlled like a zombie, and that wasn't going to happen. She walked away, muttering something in a language that reminded me of the bad guys in Lord of the Rings, and I shivered.

My mother, obviously the ringleader, came to sit beside me then, plopping down like a child on the dirt like it didn't matter if her white dress got torn or stained. I kept staring at the fire in front of me, not wanting to look at her or any of the coven members running around and packing up tents. Apparently, we were leaving in a rush.

"Do you know who that was?" she asked, leaning toward me like we were conspiring on some secret mission. I shook my head, picking at the grass. "That was my mother, your grandmother. Her name is Etain, and she is the one who discovered the wrongdoing in Azazel's judgment."

That was interesting, but I had a different question for her. "What about your father?" I watched her face from the corner of my eye and saw the aversion in her expression.

"I never knew my father. My mother told me what a horrible man he was, and that was enough for me."

"Was he a witch, or something like it?"

"No men are witches, Blair. They are sometimes sorcerers. More often, our male children have no powers, which is part of what makes you so special."

For some reason, that made me sad, and I couldn't help but ask questions I probably didn't want answered. "So, do you always send the father away? I mean, there are no men here. Do the girls stay with you and have no fathers? And what do you do with the boys? Do you send them away with their fathers and forget about them? Or do you..." I couldn't even bring myself to say the words, *kill them.*

"I didn't send you away, Blair. And many of these women have husbands at home, as well as sons." She sounded so reasonable, and I wanted to believe what she said. But I remembered how Seraphina talked about my mother and her coven, and I knew they were nothing but liars. I wasn't going to fall for any of her deceptive, loving gestures, or her cute little stories, or her looks. That had been Dad's mistake, believing that beauty meant goodness, and I wasn't going to repeat history.

I sighed and stood. "I have to take a leak. I'll be right back."

"Where are you going?" she asked sharply, moving quickly in front of me to block my path.

I stepped around her. "I'm going to a tree over there to piss. No way am I whipping out my junk in front of all these women, family or not, and that includes you." I still had my dignity, after all.

She cast a suspicious glance toward the woods but let me go. "If you aren't back in one minute, I'm coming for you."

"Well, then, it's a good thing I don't need to shit!" I called back. I stepped up to the tree and sidled around it, at least partially blocking their view of me. I unbuckled my belt and gasped as a face appeared in the bushes next to me.

"Do not move, young man," came a deep voice, so low I could barely hear him. As his features grew clearer, I was ready to run back to my mother, certain she was preferable to this red-faced monster. He reminded me of Darth Maul in Star Wars, and I was actually scared. "I'm here to help, as a favor to Seraphina."

I perked up, and while the thought of her hanging around this creep was about as comfortable as thinking of the prom queen spending time with the geeks in the library, I believed him. I nodded slightly, not saying anything, and he told me, "You will come with me, as soon as I've created a diversion for the coven."

Okay, now I was stoked. I didn't know who this guy was or what he could do, but if he was anything like Seraphina, I couldn't wait to see what sort of distraction he'd create. I stayed where I was, and as I heard footsteps coming toward me, I turned to look at my mother's angry face.

She was halfway between me and the campfire when I felt heat brush my back, and almost instantaneously, the campfire exploded. My mother was thrown forward and landed on her face as several of the other witches screamed, embers flying at them as they scrambled for safety. The tents caught fire easily, and it created a ring around the encampment, so the witches were stuck between the flames in the center and the ones around the edges. I saw my mother stand, just on the other side of the fingers of fire that made me sweat, and she stared at me, her rage filling the air.

I smirked and waved. "Adios, madre." There was a hot hand at my back, and I turned to look up at the stranger who'd just blown up the entire witch camp. "Dude, that was awesome. You've gotta teach me that trick."

He smiled, which looked really creepy on his face. "If it were my gift to give, I would. Come, we must hurry. Seraphina and your father await your safe return." He didn't tell me twice, and I ran with him, holding his hand, glancing back once at the sound of another large boom, followed by the frustrated cries of the witches.

CHAPTER TWENTY ONE

Seraphina stopped the car abruptly, and I heard the crash in the distance. "What the hell was that?" Seth asked, grabbing the backs of our seats and pulling himself forward to scan the forest in front of us.

Smoke rose from the trees about three miles down the small incline of the hill in large, heavy plumes. My heart thudded in my chest. "Tell me that wasn't the coven's camp."

"Do you want me to lie?" Seraphina asked in a deadpan tone. I turned to look at her, wondering if she was really fucking joking at a time like this, but I found her with eyes narrowed, which meant she was thinking hard.

I waited, my stomach churning, and she suddenly bolted out of the Jeep. I followed, but I couldn't keep up, and I lost her less than a thousand feet in. I wanted to holler out to her, but I didn't know if I needed to be quiet or what. Seth slammed into me, and I pushed him to the side, not wanting him to be panting in my ear as I tried to listen. I heard footsteps, approaching rather than retreating, and I squared up for a scuffle.

But through the thicker trees ahead, I saw three faces, one of which was entirely unexpected. I dropped to my knees as Blair sprinted into my arms, and I kissed his head, squeezing him so tight I probably came close to choking him out. Seraphina joined us, wrapping her arms around the boy with a smile, and Shila strode more slowly and purposefully behind them.

I looked up at him in amazement, and he shrugged. "They were preparing to move. I thought I might get him more quickly and easily than you."

I nodded in stunned silence, not knowing how to thank him, and Blair pulled away from me, his mismatched eyes sparkling with excitement. "Dad, you should have seen it! He came in and blew up the campfire, and the embers fell and burned some of the witches. And then he trapped them with more fire and burned down their tents. They were so pissed off, and it was so awesome."

Great, my son had another superhero to worship. Seraphina stood and bowed to Shila. "I am now in your debt," she told him.

But he shook his head. "Follow your destiny without question, old friend, and your debt will be repaid." He exploded and was gone, and I gaped at Seraphina.

"What does that mean?"

She shook her head, looking confused herself. "I'm not sure, but we don't have much time. We've got to get out of here before they find a way around the flames." She ushered Blair toward the edge of the woods and the Jeep, which we'd left running, and I yanked at Seth, who stood staring with a smile of appreciation on his face as he saw the smoke beginning to fill the air around us.

As I got behind the wheel, I heard Blair still chattering away at Seraphina. "I don't know how he did it, but none of the trees or bushes or anything even got singed. It was like he had some sort of force field that protected everything that didn't belong to the witches."

I saw Seraphina ruffle his hair as Seth finally arrived, and then I was gone, not even paying attention to what direction we were going. I just needed away from where we were. I thought I was probably going east, which meant I would eventually hit a road or a highway. From there, we could figure out the next step.

I glanced at the clock and cursed under my breath. Even with the help we'd had, we'd lost around three hours. I didn't complain, since I felt nothing but relief and gratitude as I saw my son in the back through the rearview mirror, but it was frustrating. We were never going to make our destination if we kept getting held up, or chased, or kidnapped.

"You'll hit 601 eventually," Seth piped up, and I looked at him to see him checking the map. "Take it south, and you'll hit 60 again. We can speed across that for a while and make up a little lost time before we get back on a smaller road, like 70."

I just nodded. I didn't know highways like the wrinkles on my balls the way Seth did, and I trusted him to get us where we needed to be. I met Blair's eyes in the mirror. "Are you okay? Are you hurt at all?"

He shook his head. "Not physically. I might be traumatized, though, after that little family reunion." He smirked. "No twelve year old should have to meet a gaggle of witches that include his psycho bitch mother and his ranting lunatic grandmother, who wanders around speaking in the language of Mordor. If I'd have stayed much longer, I might have had to change my name to Precious."

I laughed. I couldn't believe my son had a

sense of humor about all this. But mostly, I laughed because I seethed inside and was trying to maintain the appearance of calm sanity. "Did she say anything that bothered you in particular?" I knew she had to have spouted fallacies like sunflower seed shells.

He squirmed, and Seraphina put an arm around his shoulders. "Whatever it is, even if it has to do with one or all of us, we won't be upset with you, Blair." I caught her pointed look in the mirror and gave her a short nod.

He sighed. "She said a lot of things I don't believe, a lot about loving you and choosing you because she met a lot of angels and you were the only one she was attracted to. She said you took me, not because you were afraid for me, but because you were afraid that I would love her more than you." He shook his head and gazed at his hands. I felt terrible; the bitch had done a number on her. "She's just…she sucks, Dad."

I didn't have an answer, but Seth did. "That is the biggest understatement I think I've ever heard, kid. The woman is poison."

"What if I'm like her, Dad? I have her genes. I saw her eyes."

"You've already proven otherwise," Seraphina broke in. "You are a good person, Blair, and someone who starts out as good as you cannot be turned into that sort of monster." I saw him look up at her, and she winked down at him. "Besides, if you ever had a thought even close to being as nasty as hers, I'd turn you over my lap and paddle it out of you myself."

He smiled, and so did I. Seraphina, despite my misgivings, was turning out to be a godsend, and I scowled at the term even as I thought it. I didn't like thinking about religious and spirituality, but it sounded like I didn't have much choice in the matter anymore. I was the product of heavenly creatures, and I had to recognize that somehow.

The drive began to wear on me about two hours in, and though we were back on real roads, my body ached and my head throbbed. When my stomach growled, so did I and I asked Seraphina, "What happened to that food you prepared this morning?"

Within seconds, I was handed a tortilla containing a mixture of meat and cheese and veggies, and I devoured it in about four bites. She handed me a second, and I ate it more slowly, tasting it this time. She passed out food to Seth and Blair, too, and I saw her nibble on some of it herself.

"We can't drive all night," Seth said through a yawn. "I know it's early in the day still, but we've got to plan ahead. Being out at night is a no-go, and besides, we all need the rest."

I agreed, but I was still reluctant to stop. "Maybe if we go somewhere a little out of the way, it would be better. Harder for our stalkers to find us." They would be out of the fire by now, and I could just imagine the rabid behavior of a bunch of angry witches who'd been deterred by an unknown source.

Without hesitation, Seth pulled out the map and started searching for a good place to stay the night. He frowned and traced some lines with his fingers. "Well, we're headed straight to Roswell right now. We could see about sneaking into Area 51 and settling into a damn spaceship." I smacked his arm, and he chuckled. "Or we could head south to Carlsbad and cross into Texas. We should be able to make Midland in time to camp out or get a hotel."

I nixed the idea of camping again. It was too dangerous to be outdoors. I at least needed the warning of a door opening before someone tried to snatch Blair again. "We'll get a motel room. In fact, call ahead and make reservations."

He arched a brow at me. "I need signal for that. In case you haven't noticed, we're in the ass crack of the world right now. I'll call when we get to Roswell." With a plan, I felt a little better. I could tell I was headed towards the bowels of depression, and that wouldn't do any of us any good. I could be a mean son of a bitch when I wasn't happy, and this was a bad time for it.

We weren't going to hit any notable hole-in-the-wall towns before Roswell, but at least the scenery wasn't as bland, since we must have passed every fucking national forest in the state on the way. We were just about on fumes when we rolled into the strange, alien-themed city, and this time, I didn't let Blair out of sight. We went into a grocery store to use the bathroom, where there were multiple stalls so he wouldn't freak out about privacy, and just to stretch our legs, I gave him twenty bucks and let him go into one of the souvenir shops with Seraphina.

He came out with a tub of green gook labeled 'alien slime' and a hat that said 'I got abducted, what's your excuse?' Seth elbowed me. "Your son's a smartass."

I pressed my lips together. "Tell me something I don't know." I slapped Blair on the back. "Are you ready to get back on the road?"

"Sure. But when all this is over, we've got to take a vacation here. Who knows? If there are angels and witches, there are probably aliens, too."

"Yeah, well, just because something exists doesn't mean I want to stare it in its seven eyes," I told him. Seraphina grabbed my arm, stopping me from getting back in the Jeep.

I gave her a questioning look. "Are you alright?" I must have looked confused because she shrugged. "I know you were beside yourself with worry, and it can't be easy for you to have hidden that woman from him all this time, only to have him finally meet her and see the reason you made that choice."

She had a point, but honestly, I was glad of that aspect of things. "Now he knows. He's seen for himself what a piece of work she is, and he won't have any delusions that he's missing out on a mother's love by not knowing her." I felt my jaw muscle twitching; it was a very uncomfortable topic for me.

Her hand crept up my arm and then skimmed down over my chest. "This will be over soon, you know. And I intend to assure we have a happy ending." Her spirit was so strong, her outlook so positive. I couldn't imagine the things she'd seen in her experience, and to maintain such a demeanor was beyond my comprehension. Without thinking, I reached up and smoothed a tendril of curly blond hair behind her ear, finding the skin their soft and warm.

"We all need companionship, Jax," she whispered, her expression somber, and then she was walking away, jumping into the Jeep with Blair and playing with the nasty green goo. My crotch ached, and I adjusted my jeans before settling back in.

Seth gave me a knowing look, and I growled at him, daring him to say something. He played it smart and simply pointed me in the right direction.

CHAPTER TWENTY TWO

Midland turned out to be a good choice. The motel was clean, and the area was as sparse and dry as the country we'd covered so far. Blair was huddled in the desk chair, playing his PSP, which I hadn't even realized he packed, since this was the first time on the trip it had appeared, and Seth had his cell phone out, checking various accounts and who knew what else.

I'd told Blair that, if he got up early in the morning, he could shower then, since I wasn't thrilled at the thought of running out of hot water. I was already waiting for Seraphina to finish so I could hop in, and I'd probably have to wash military style – in and out in less than three minutes – if I didn't want to freeze. I stood against the wall, my head leaned back, waiting for the door to open, and when it did, I turned toward it, bumping hard against Seraphina's body.

With her hair wet and her scent mixed with the floral aroma of the shampoo, I felt drugged, the sensation heady, and I had to catch my balance with a hand on the door frame. She bit her lip and said, "I'm sorry."

I shook my head. "No worries. Did you leave me any hot water?"

She shrugged playfully. "If you were worried about it…" She didn't finish the sentence, and I was shocked to see her blush as she looked back toward the bathroom and the steam inside. Had she really just flirted with me, with Blair and Seth both in the room? Impressive.

I leaned in toward her. "I'll take that as an invitation and remember the warning next time." She ducked away from me, and I watched her flop down on one of the beds and grab the television remote before I slipped into the bathroom to clean the dirt and dust off myself.

Fortunately, this motel had their boilers turned up, and I reveled in the feel of the scalding water for a couple of minutes before scrubbing down. I sighed as the itch of the road dust and dried sweat disappeared, and I felt like I'd just cleaned a bunch of cobwebs out of my brain. As I stepped out, I thought about the day ahead.

If we managed to stay on track without distractions, we could be in New Orleans around nightfall, and this whole dramatic flight could end, as long as Seraphina wasn't mistaken in her understanding of the prophecy. It wasn't going to be easy; we were passing a lot of tourist attractions along the way, whichever route we took, and Blair was going to want to see everything. I had to admit, it would be fun, and I was more than tempted to promise we'd do the sightseeing on the way home.

But I didn't want to think about the possibility of failure to return, so I kept that idea to myself.

Besides, I figured Seraphina might be good to babysit for a night while Seth and I went out to the French Quarter and celebrated before we left New Orleans. We would definitely need a few drinks at that point.

I toweled off and pulled on the only pair of pants that weren't jeans Seth had grabbed for me. I guess he hadn't planned for such a FUBAR situation as this. The jogging pants were old but comfortable, and I grabbed the T-shirt from the counter before stepping out into the room with the two queen sized beds, where I found Seth and Seraphina bantering over the TV.

"Seriously, Blondie, you'll never make it to the runway. Even in six-inch heels, you're lacking about six inches to qualify."

She pouted at him. "You know, it's not very nice to ruin my dreams just because you don't want to watch America's Next Top Model reruns. I wouldn't tell you that you'll never be a movie star or a superhero because you want to watch Thor, which you've probably already seen fifty times."

He grunted. "I'm already a superhero, woman. I have unnatural strength and speed and brains."

She nodded. "I can't speak to the strength and speed, but I hesitate to validate the brains, Forrest Gump."

I laughed and intervened. "Why don't we settle this the easy way? I think we should get to bed because we've got an early morning and a long drive tomorrow."

"That works for me," Seraphina said, turning the tube off as she hopped off the bed.

Seth stared at the two beds, and I could read his mind, mostly because I had the same question. What would the sleeping arrangements be?

Blair stretched as he turned off his game and laid on the bed nearest the door. "Nope," I told him. "I want you on the inside, away from the doors and windows." He rolled his eyes at me, but he must have been too tired to argue, getting up and stumbling to the other bed. He fell facedown, and I think he was asleep instantly. I glanced at Seraphina, a sudden desire to hold her through the night flowing rampant in my veins, but I didn't say anything aloud.

Seth had some shit to say, though. "You know, based on weight and size, even distribution puts you in bed with the kid and Goldilocks with me."

"In your dreams," Seraphina shot him down instantly. "Your ego would take up my entire side of the bed." She met my gaze and hesitated before saying quietly, "I'll sleep with Blair. You're brothers. I'm sure you've shared a bed before."

Was that a hint of regret in her tone, or was it my imagination? Either way, I was going to be stuck sharing a mattress with my brother, who tended to flail his limbs during the night. If I didn't get enough sleep, that bastard was going to be the one driving in the morning. Reluctantly, I moved to the other bed, taking the side nearest the door, and secured the dart gun under my pillow.

Seth grumbled as he crawled in beside me. "I swear to god, if I wake up to you humping my leg, or you accidently dart me, I'm going to have your ass in the morning." I ignored him in favor of watching Seraphina curl in next to my son. It was a nice image to keep in my mind after the lights went out and I fell asleep.

***

"Hey, Dad, when this is all over, we're not moving to a place like this," Blair yawned at me as we loaded up the car to leave the next morning. He looked around at what was the Midland-Odessa basin with a disgusted look. "Everything looks the same in the daylight as it did in the dark last night. There's nothing to see."

I couldn't have agreed more. When the witch-bitches had no more use for us, I was done with deserts. I wanted lush, green lands and trees, maybe by a lake. I had a feeling Blair would argue with me, wanting to go back to Nevada, but we could find some sort of compromise. I was convinced.

"Well, kiddo, you've got a lot of optimism going for you there," Seth piped up, and I shot him a dirty look. I didn't need him getting an 'all hope is lost' attitude now, especially in front of my son. After all, we'd come this far, overcome some definite against-all-odds situations, and were on the brink of victory. There would be no more running, no more hiding, and no more looking over our shoulders. Blair would be free of the burden I'd inadvertently placed on him.

I had to believe we'd triumph. It was the only way to maintain my sanity. We had a little over twelve hours of driving ahead, and I knew we wouldn't make it nonstop. And we weren't taking the scenic route; Seraphina believed the witches would stick to the woods, having lost their camp and many of their magical pieces, and we would make far better time on the main road. That was the important thing, and just between Seth and me, we'd decided we would be better off hiding in plain sight. We didn't think the witches wanted to alert the general public to what they had in store for the world. They would have an uprising on their hands.

"Alright, guys, lock and load. We're not stopping until we get to Dallas." I made the announcement as Seth threw the last of the things we'd bothered to unpack into the cargo trunk of the Jeep. "I hope you have snacks."

"How far is that, Dad?" Blair asked, grabbing his backpack and digging through about a million granola bars, candy packages, and other miscellaneous snacks he'd collected.

"It's five hours," Seth answered for me as he hopped into the passenger seat. "But I bet your father's lead foot is going to get us there in four."

I rolled my eyes. "Hi, Pot. I'm Kettle, and you're black."

"You know, it doesn't do us any good to go faster if you demolish the car and we never get there," Blair snipped with a cocky smirk.

"Thank you, Captain Sunshine! I'm not going to get us killed. You've been riding with the two of us driving for twelve years, and we haven't even had a close call."

Seth cleared his throat. "Well, there was the one time…"

"Shut up!" I smacked the back of his head.

"I think we should all stop fighting and get on the road," Seraphina piped up, the first thing she'd said through the entire bantering conversation. "If there's concern about the drivers we're discussing, I could drive."

"No!" Suddenly, as my brother chorused in with me, I didn't hate him so much. We were both control freaks and had to deal with each other, but no way were we going to give up control to someone else. At least, not in terms of being behind the wheel. I might give Seraphina a chance to take control in the bedroom. I could imagine the beautiful things she could do to me.

I revved the Jeep's engine to cover how revved my own was, and I checked to make sure everyone was buckled in before taking off. I was on the road and gunning for Dallas, and no one was going to get in my way. It really sucked being on the side of good sometimes there were far more people willing to back the bad guys against us, and we were only four. Technically, I didn't want to count Blair, but then again, I supposed he was the one with the power. And besides, Seraphina might count for more than one, with all her cool little tricks.

It was somewhere around Sweetwater I realized we were not the team with the advantage, and I was suddenly terrified about losing Blair, but not just about my son. I had three other people with me that mattered to me, not one, and the idea of losing any of them in this battle made me nauseous.

I pulled over at a park and told Seth, "No one leaves the car." I jumped out and ran, emptying my stomach with violent wretches behind the nearest large tree. Gasping for air, I wiped my mouth on the hem of my shirt and stared off at nothing. I knew I'd been in denial about Seth for years. I'd told myself he was my brother and I loved him, but if I had to sacrifice him to keep my son alive, I could handle that. Now I knew better, because the idea of going on without him literally terrified me, and I wasn't afraid of anything.

But the real surprise to me came at the thought of Seraphina getting hurt in all of this. I didn't know if she was immortal or what, but you learn through the years that even immortality comes with fine print. I was sure she could be destroyed somehow, and that idea alone had me gagging again. There was nothing in my stomach, so I managed to control myself, but it was only by pure will.

"Are you alright?" I whirled at Seraphina's voice, ready to rage at her for getting out of the car against my orders, but she was nowhere to be seen. I craned my neck and found her still sitting in the back seat, though her eyes were closed, and her voice carried in a whisper on the wind.

I clenched my jaw, remembering she was an air elemental. But I spoke in return, feeling really stupid, like I was talking to myself in this damned place. I kept it to a whisper, hoping she could bring it back to her on the wind. I didn't need the rest of my family accusing me of insanity because they thought I was suddenly chatting at some damn ghost even they couldn't see. "I'm fine, I just felt sick for a minute."

"I can see that," her voice swirled around me on a breeze that smelled like spring blossoms on a cherry tree. It was a scent I hadn't smelled in twelve years, and it went a long way in settling my stomach. "You aren't car sick, so what caused this?"

I leaned back against the tree and closed my eyes, facing away from the Jeep and muttered, "It's not important."

"Don't hold yourself at a lower value than others," she chided, the scent growing stronger as she lectured me. "If you're ill, or upset, it's just as important as anyone else in our party feeling the same way. Tell me why you've vomited."

I made a face. I wish she hadn't known what happened. Losing your stomach was a sign of weakness, and for some reason, I never wanted Seraphina to see me as weak. What would she think if I told her the truth? I sighed, the aroma so strong it made me lightheaded, and I found myself telling her, "If anyone gets hurt or dies in this task, I'm not sure I can make it."

"Of course you can," she replied matter-of-factly. "You're a very strong man, and you must persevere. At the same time, you should be more confident. No matter what we face, the odds are in our favor. We have the Sacred Key, and it will remain so."

So she had more faith in my strength, and in our ability to succeed, than I did. That was good to know. "Sera, I can't lose my son. And I can't ask you to risk yourself to save him."

There was no response, no breeze, and I

winced. I shouldn't have said anything. Then, a soft wisp of air brushed over my cheek. "You are concerned for my well-being. That is sweet." I sighed again, and she told me, "You have not asked anything of me. It is my will and my devotion to be here and to do what I can to help. I don't wish to lose anyone, either, Jax, least of all you."

My eyes popped open as the scent of blossoms turned to sugar and cinnamon and her words struck me deep inside. I heard a bubbly giggle on a wayward breeze as well. "Sera is a name I like, that you may call me."

I couldn't help but smile. "Yes, well, you piss me off again, and we're going back to Finny, got it?"

"It's a deal. Now, we need to get back on the road and get to Dallas. Do you need someone else to drive?"

I thought about it for a moment. I didn't want to hand the wheel over to Seth; he was already going to give me hell for stopping when I'd been so adamant about not doing so. And

Seraphina's driving skills were questionable at best. I assessed my stomach and decided I could drive. "I'll be fine." I stood straight, and feeling a bit sentimental, I told her, "Thank you."

"There is no need for thanks," she whispered back, and I felt a brush across my lips as I strode back to the Jeep. I touched them with my fingertips and saw the ghost of a smile on her face as I approached. I winked at her and swung back into the driver's seat.

"So much for the road warrior," Seth taunted. "I like your idea of a nonstop trip, brother. I think you might need to check the dictionary for a definition of the term."

"The only reason I need a dictionary is to swing and crush your face with it," I growled back. "We can't plan everything, you know."

"I don't accept that," he argued, sounding offended. Of course, Seth was the king of having plans A through H for every situation. "You could have drank less water this morning, and you wouldn't have needed to take a leak."

I was almost relieved that's what he assumed I'd been doing. "Hey, Seth, eat shit and die." I pulled back on the highway, promising myself I wouldn't stop again, and that I wouldn't let my panic cause me to get sick again.

CHAPTER TWENTY THREE

Dallas was a foodie town, and by the time we got there, the traffic sucked and we were all ravenous. You could only eat so many granola bars without something to drink before they started to scratch and cut your mouth. My only debate was whether to get Mexican food or stop at some hole in the wall barbecue joint.

We ended up at a small cantina, with some of the best flautas I'd ever eaten in my life and salsa with flavor that burst in my mouth like fireworks. We ate like crazy, and I knew, after a meal like that and lots to drink, getting back on the road right away would only mean stopping again before we even made it to Tyler, much less to the Louisiana border.

So, I made sure we toiled around for a bit after we ate, headed to a gas station to fuel up, and sat in the sun for a little longer. Seth grew impatient, but the truth was, we were going to arrive after dark anyway, and it was my experience that witches were more active after dark, stronger. It didn't matter if we got to New Orleans and this portal at nine o'clock or three in the morning. We were facing the same odds.

I sat on the hood of the Jeep, one leg stretched out and the other bent at the knee so I could rest my arm on it. I squinted into the bright sunshine still not at its peak and watched as Sera strolled with Blair back and forth along the fence across the street. She made sure never to take him out of my sight and to keep him on the side of her away from the road, which I greatly appreciated.

The more I evaluated their relationship, the guiltier I felt. If I'd given him a mother –

somehow – along the way, Blair would have been a lot more normal. As it was, his restlessness had seemed to settle down over the last couple of days, which totally went against everything bred into him. He was always ready for adventure and grew almost obnoxious at times like this.

They stopped walking and faced away from me, watching the llamas and cows grazing in the field beyond, and I nearly choked on overwhelming emotion as my son leaned his head against Sera's shoulder. I wasn't particularly affectionate with my son physically, but I felt like I'd done my share of hugging, kissing, and tussling his hair over the years. But at this moment, I realized how starved he must be for a truly nurturing hand, and as Sera put her arm around his shoulders to draw him closer, I had to turn away.

If there hadn't been anything else attractive about her, or she hadn't been the loyal, kind, and likeable individual she was, I would have loved her for giving my son something he desperately needed that I couldn't. As it was, there was so much more to her than a kind soul and a delicious body.

I was reminded of my insatiable desire for Amelia as I stared at Sera intently, my need for her double that former desire. I wouldn't have thought it possible, but it was like someone had finally flipped a magnet inside me that was pushing her away with a strong sense of purpose, and now, I was drawn to her with irresistible force.

I strolled across the road, which was little more than a driveway, and joined them beside the fence. I stepped up beside Blair, putting a hand on his head to share the moment, and Sera shifted, pushing my son forward so he stood in front of us and leaned back into us. Then, she snaked her arm around my waist, and I just stood there, accepting her silent request, as if we'd just signed a contract to make her officially part of the family.

So many thoughts slammed to the front of my brain that, even if Blair hadn't been right there, I wouldn't have been able to tell Sera what I felt at that exact moment. All I knew was that, right or wrong, she felt good at my side, and I wanted her to stay there, for my own satisfaction as well as to give my son the tender guidance every boy needed.

"Every species, in this realm and the others, are very different," Sera said quietly, and I didn't move, wanting to hear every word. "The vastness of individuality doesn't stop with the person but continues with the entire species. When those of us who are so different take on a form like yours, we join a global community that breathes the same air, eats of the same organic material, and sleeps with the same type of brainwaves. Creatures of the heaven, the earth, and the below, whether magical or not, are much less different than they seem on the surface, when you really dig to the bottom of the source of energy within us all."

"So, you don't look like this most of the time, huh?" Blair asked without turning around. I stared at Sera, waiting for her answer. I had a very different take on what she was trying to say, and I needed to know if she was going to explain it or just give Blair some brush-off answer.

"No, I don't. In my natural form, I'm little more than energy, like the movement of the wind. I can take many forms, from that of a dust devil or tornado to a large flying bird to this human body you see here." She smiled, and I wanted to touch the body that didn't really belong to her, kiss the lips she'd formed for herself. "In this vessel, I'm susceptible to things which would otherwise fail to affect me. I'm still far stronger than any human, but I'm also vulnerable to attack."

I winced at the confirmation that Sera wasn't invincible. It was just one more worry I had to deal with through this whole debacle. I reminded myself that I had to focus on the priority, which was much more important than any of our lives. The important thing was to make sure Azazel didn't get his hands on my son and make his way into heaven. If he did, more than our little party would suffer the consequences.

When the hell had the fate of the world fallen

on our shoulders?

I smiled to myself, thinking Seth would tell me it had happened the day I'd let a fucking skirt get the best of me, back in high school. I wondered if he would think any better of Sera, now that she'd proven herself to be a true ally. Maybe he'd finally approve of a woman in my life.

Not that I expected Sera to be a part of *my* life, exactly. But standing here, with her arm around me and Blair in front of us, I knew she had to be part of my son's, and that brought her into mine by extension.

Sera spoke again, drawing me out of my really disturbing thoughts. "The point is, in the end, we are all driven by the same life force, and we are not so different." I turned and found her staring directly at me, and I locked gazes with those incredible golden eyes. Something caught in my throat, and I had an overwhelming wave of emotion sweep through me, the likes of which I'd felt only once in my life – the first time I'd stared into my son's mismatched eyes.

I stepped back from the two of them, just looking at their dynamic, and I swear Sera read my mind. I could see my thoughts reflected in her eyes, or so it seemed. Unable to discuss the possibility with her while Blair was right here – and until I knew I wouldn't lose her – I cleared my throat and broke eye contact. "I think it's time to get back on the road, guys. We've hung around long enough."

Blair was reluctant, and I couldn't blame him. In his position, I would want to crawl in a hole and stay there; waiting until some other dope like me fell for an evil witch and had a child they could use. But he squared his shoulders and strode across the street and hopped in the Jeep.

"He's not frightened," Sera said quietly as we waited for a car to pass. "He only wanted to stay and watch the animals for a time. They calmed him."

"If he's not scared, why does he need to be calmed?" I asked, disgruntled that my son was being forced into this position.

"He's excited, Jax. He has a mission, a purpose, and in his mind he's like the superhero who's going to save the world. What could be better to a twelve-year-old boy?"

I could think of lots of things – not *having* to save the world, maybe not having to see and talk to ghosts, having a girlfriend and a permanent home. But I didn't say any of those things, instead taking her hand and pulling her across the street. Seth was settling himself behind the wheel, and I didn't care. I needed to give up some of my control, and a bit of my sense of responsibility with it.

"Hey, fathead, are we geared up?" he asked.

"Sure, pencil-dick. Next stop is Shreveport. I'll give you permission to drive fast, as long as you keep it at a safe level and don't get stopped." I didn't want my brother whining about speed limits, and I didn't want to have to stay alert about traffic and the road. We were three hours from the Louisiana border, and with Seth driving more like he preferred, we'd make it in just fewer than two and a half.

That was enough time to let my mind truly wander, and I felt I could be more prepared when we reached the portal.

"You got it, bro." He looked in the rearview mirror with a smirk. "Hey, Airbender, are you buckled up, or do you even need to be?"

I turned back to see an amused expression on Sera's face, and she raised an eyebrow as she quipped, "I am, but I'm prepared to save our lives if you decide to drive us into oncoming traffic or hit a pothole. I'm alert and aware, oh, mighty headstrong driver."

I expected Seth to get snarky, but he just laughed. "Then away we go."

I leaned back in my seat and got as comfortable as I could. After all, Jeeps were made to be rugged and useful, not exactly catering to a luxury ride. I reached for the radio and cranked up the rock music, needing something as background noise to help clear my head. We were headed straight into the fire; I could feel it in my bones, and we weren't prepared for what we were going to face. I had some idea of my ex-wife's capabilities, and I'd seen a modicum of what her entire coven could do, but with the backing of another entity like Azazel, there was no telling how powerful they could be.

I was fast, and I was strong. Seth was smart and also had some unbelievable strength. Sera had the wind at her back, literally, and at this point, I wouldn't put it past her to call in some more favors, if necessary. And though Blair was still young and small and didn't seem to manifest the powers Seth and I had come into shortly after puberty yet, he was determined, and he was the central piece of our puzzle.

But all that added up to shits and giggles if we faced a legion of witches and a dark power that was millenniums old. I scrubbed a hand over my face, trying to think of some kind of strategy that would give us the upper hand. The element of surprise would have been good. Even better would be arriving ahead of the bad guys. I no longer had any faith that we had either advantage working for us.

I considered asking Sera if there was another portal. Maybe, if we let them think we were still headed to New Orleans and quickly managed to turn another way, to a portal that wasn't too far away, we could escape notice long enough to get the job done. But I doubted, having already come halfway across the country, there would be anything close enough to make the sprint and succeed.

I heard my son start to wail and cry in the back seat, his singing voice somewhat lacking, and I laughed. In the midst of everything so desperately fucked, he still found joy where he could. I supposed Seth and I could take a lesson from him, and I smacked my brother's arm with the back of my hand to catch his attention. When he glanced at me, I started singing along, prompting him to join in. The cacophony of all of our voices left a lot to be desired, but I was determined that we were going to be happy up to the last minute. I hadn't given my son nearly as much joy in his life as he deserved, no matter how hard I tried, and from this point forward, that was going to change.

CHAPTER TWENTY FOUR

"You can't bring me here, have me stop the car, and expect me not to play a couple of machines," Seth argued emphatically.

I should have known better. In Nevada, Seth had spent what little free time he had in the casinos, and now, as the light of day began to dim and gave over to the brilliance of the small Sin City in Shreveport, the call of the slots was too much for him to resist. I didn't want us separated for any amount of time, but I wasn't going to take my son into a damn casino. I had a feeling we'd have our asses kicked right out, which would only draw more attention to us.

Sera put her hands on her hips. "I'm sorry, Jax. Your brother has severe impulse control problems, and he apparently can't manage a premature evacuation." I held back a snort. "If he insists on being immature and giving into his baser needs, he obviously needs a babysitter. Why don't you put gas in the car and find us some food, and I'll follow the man with the dollar signs for eyes to make sure he doesn't get into too much trouble."

"See, Jax? I always told you I was the more desirable one. I get to escort the lovely lady into the casino and look like a pimp."

I grunted. "She's escorting you, asshole. And she's going to make sure you spend no more than fifteen minutes. We need to eat and get back on the road." I didn't really care about getting back on the road as much as reuniting our team – we were obviously stronger together – but I didn't want to say anything in front of Blair to make him nervous, and I knew Seth would take to the request to get going again better than what he would consider an insult to his strength.

"You worry too much," he grumbled, sounding like a small child. I rolled my eyes as he even dragged his toe in the dirt. My brother could be such a pathetic infant when he didn't get his way. I was sure that, without Sera's supervision, he'd play for hours and lose his ass, simply because we had the money to lose.

Instead of trying to address him, I turned to Sera. "Fifteen minutes, okay? When time's up, you text me from his phone and tell me which casino you're in. I'll meet you at the front door."

She nodded and held out her hand to Seth. "Come on, sweetheart, let's take care of your addiction so we can move on." He seemed to get a bit of a pick-me-up from holding her hand, and I watched them with a modicum of jealousy as they walked away. It looked like he was headed to Harrah's, but I couldn't be sure.

"You don't hide your feelings very well, Dad,"

Blair told me, his brows drawn tightly together. "It's not like Seraphina has any interest in Uncle Seth."

I bonked him on the back of his head. "Mind your own business," I told him.

He smiled. "I would love to, but you can't seem to mind yours. Why don't you just tell her you like her and get it over with?"

We climbed back in the Jeep to find a gas station. "What makes you think I like her, anyway?"

"Oh, please! Your jaw muscle was twitching a mile a minute as soon as she held his hand. Besides, I'd have to be blind not to notice the way you look at her all the time." He sighed heavily. "You're hopeless, you know."

"I'm not hopeless," I argued, but he was probably right. I didn't want to make anything clear, at least, not until we were finished with our journey. And if we came through the other side, I still didn't know if I could speak my feelings. I was traumatized from the only relationship I'd ever had, and even though I knew Sera was nothing like Amelia, I couldn't get past the thought of getting burnt again. It was so asinine…all the strength and power in the world didn't give me confidence in my own ability to maintain a healthy romantic relationship.

I practically attached Blair to my hip while I filled the gas tank and again when we entered to pick up some convenience store food. I wanted to ralph some more at the thought of eating greasy hot dogs and potato chips again, but it was sustenance, and as soon as all of this was over, we were going to a steakhouse to celebrate.

The text came through just as we were settling in the Jeep, and I swung back to Jack Binion's to find Sera and Seth waiting for us. Seth had a shit-eating grin, and even Sera smiled ruefully. "Go ahead, champ, tell them what you won."

Seth beamed at me as he buckled his seatbelt. "Jax, I have to say, our little air goddess is a good luck charm. I played three games and doubled my money every game. I spent more time cashing in than playing."

At least he'd had a good run. "So, what did you end up with?" I asked, not really wanting to know.

"I started with five hundred and left with four grand. I'm telling you, this one's got good karma or something." He poked a finger in Sera's direction, and I looked at her through the rearview mirror. She winked and shook her head as if denying she'd had anything to do with it. I had to wonder, though. Who wouldn't?

Blair passed out food, and I swallowed mine as fast as I could, the taste making me want to gag. I downed my soda to wash it away, and we were back on the highway, headed down 49 on the last leg to New Orleans. It was just a little over 300 miles, and I knew I could make it in under five hours, though the last few miles would have to be traversed under Sera's direction, since I had no idea where the portal was.

We rode in silence as the sun set behind us,

and my nerves began to eat away at me. I assumed everyone else had the same problem, so I didn't even bother trying to strike up idle conversation. Blair pulled out his PSP, the quiet sound effects fading away in the air blowing through the Jeep as I drove a little faster than even I intended. Fear drove me, made my foot heavier. Unlike some people, I didn't freeze when I was frightened; I wanted to remove the threat, so I sped up the pace.

As we drew close to the city of black magic and ghosts, I felt a bit uncomfortable, wondering how inundated we would be by the spirits. I worried mostly about Blair, his sensitivity to them so potent I could only imagine how many of them would try to talk to him. It would be an unwelcome distraction this night.

But I also started to think about Mom and Dad. I hadn't seen them in years, and I wondered if they ever moved on. All the secrets they'd kept in that hidden room were mine now, and it seemed, from my perspective, they should have been allowed back into heaven. They'd paid their dues on earth, and they'd lost their mortal lives without sin, as far as I knew. But who could really tell?

Stream of consciousness brought me around to what heaven would look like. Would I even get to see it? And if so, would I see my parents again? Maybe only Blair would be allowed to enter. Or maybe, the whole plan would fail, and the prophecy wouldn't be true at all. If all of this was for nothing, I was going to be one pissed off son of a bitch, and whatever angel I could curse, I would.

Fifteen miles from I-10, Sera leaned forward. "We're going to Erzulies, a voodoo shop on Royal Street."

It was such a precise location – and such an odd choice of places to hide a portal to the upper realms – that I frowned at her. "That doesn't sound very heavenly to me," I told her, suddenly skeptical.

"All magic can be used to advantage," she replied skeptically. "Voodoo is a dark art, but surrounding a portal to the heavens in such darkness especially helps keep evil off the scent. While there are few ways to access the gate, it's essential to provide as little motivation as possible to those who would try to enter without welcome."

That made enough sense to keep me from asking any more questions. Seth already had out his phone, using GPS to find the shop and route us the rest of the way. "So, are we just going to walk in and say, hey, we're looking for the gate to heaven, can you tell us which pin cushion guards it?"

"No, we may not need to go in at all," Sera said. "The portal is accessed through several corridors underground, and while we can get there from within the store, we may escape more notice if we could park down the street, sneak into the alley, and drop through one of the manholes."

"Oh, my god, you're talking about going into the sewers in New Orleans. Have you lost your fucking mind?" Seth accused, his eyes wide. "Do you know the nasty, horrible things that go on in that city? I mean, between hurricanes, Mardi Gras, and the usual drunks, those sewers are full of everything that could possibly be noxious and toxic."

"Poor Seth is going to get his tie dirty. Maybe we should just forget the whole thing," Sera teased.

"I'm not worried about dirty. I'm worried about toxic waste. Have you ever seen the Teenage Mutant Ninja Turtles? That shit is terrifying."

"I'll let you know if I see you turn green from something other than nausea," Blair laughed from the back seat. I laughed with him, especially as Seth seemed to already be suffering from absolute disgust at the prospect of crawling through what might even be a filthier underground than New York.

"If we can't get in that way, how hard is it going to be to enter the store and go down from there?" I asked. I wanted the backup plan to be as solid as the initial plan.

"Well, I can get us in without a problem. One

thing about voodoo priestesses is that they respect my kind. Of course, some of them also try to get in the good graces of witches, so it's a little dangerous. At the same time, she'll cooperate with me, whether it's to help or to usher us right into the hands of the enemy."

"Oh, that's reassuring," Seth muttered. I gave him a sharp look, and he pressed his lips together into a thin line as he pointed to an exit sign, showing our exit was half a mile away.

The streets were still busy, and I had to count the days in my head. It was Friday, so the revelers made sense. They did us a favor in allowing us to blend in a little better. At least we wouldn't be the only people roaming the streets this late. But they also caused a problem, since it would also be easy enough for the witches to blend in, as long as they didn't stare me directly in the eyes. I didn't like it, but we had to go through this.

I followed Sera's directions until we had passed the store, and we parked in a small lot about two blocks away. The streets were littered with people and trash from a night of carousing and letting loose, and we walked the first block on the main street, under the lights that kept the French Quarter from reaching a level of creepy I wouldn't have been able to handle. At least, with the street lights, I could use my eyes to keep track of the people around us.

But as we crossed to the alley between blocks, the light died, and we were in complete darkness. I took Blair's hand and whispered, "Link hands in a chain." I felt silly whispering, but it just seemed the right thing to do under the circumstances. In the lead, I could let my enemy radar loose and know if something threatening was in front of us.

I didn't feel anything, but I didn't know if I should be relieved that we'd made it here safe and ahead of the other team, or if I should be even more terrified because they'd managed to cloak themselves so well. I didn't put anything past Amelia and her gaggle of grotesque goons, and I'd been certain they would arrive first and set a trap. The more I thought about it, the more I felt like we'd already stepped onto the net, and they were going to yank us into the air any minute.

Sera brushed a thought through my head on a soft puff of air. *This way isn't safe. Let's go to the front and go inside.*

I didn't know if it would be any safer, but I certainly preferred the road more traveled at this point. I turned around, pulling the train with me, and as we reached the corner, I ran smack into something solid but invisible. There was a blinding beam of light, and suddenly, a man stood before me.

From the tormented expression he wore and the way he eyed Blair behind me, this had to be Azazel.

CHAPTER TWENTY FIVE

"Fancy meeting you here," he spoke, and though his volume was low, his voice was piercing, resonating off every surface around us and reverberating in my ears painfully. His pitch was high, his voice carrying a bit of a whine, but to stare at him was to stare at the perfectly constructed male.

It was probably the first time in my entire life I'd felt inadequate in comparing myself to someone else. Azazel's face was pristine, even after so much time spent being tormented. I wondered if there were scars beneath the deep red armor he wore, but I didn't think it would help us at all to ask him such a question.

"Don't play games, Azazel," Sera demanded, stepping up beside me. I was swallowed by fear for her in that moment, but I could feel her strength and sense her resolve. She was more than capable of standing up to the angel who'd been tossed from heaven, and I was going to let her do her business without my input, unless I saw her about to get hurt.

"Step away, Elemental. I have no quarrel with you." He wrinkled his nose in a sneer, and he pointed at my son, whose body tensed. He was probably thinking of all the same unsavory things that I wanted to say to this beast. "In fact, we have no quarrel at all, as long as you bring me the boy."

I scoffed. "Do you really think I'm just going to hand over my son to you so you can climb the stairs and strike down every heavenly being? You've been down in that pit of yours too long and you've started to lose lucidity. Think again, asshole. You can't have my son."

He crossed his arms over his chest and began

to pace back and forth. I would have stricken him down, had I thought I would make any progress in doing so. But I had a feeling that any sort of violence would start a war, so I waited to hear his thoughts. "Well, I admit, I thought this might be difficult. I imagined you'd have just as adamant an attitude as your late mother did. It was such a pity to see her life stamped out so early. But it had to be done when she refused to help me. She was too pure for this world anyway. All I did was send her home."

Seth took a threatening step forward. "You killed our parents?" he raged.

I put a hand on his chest, knowing if I didn't calm him down, he'd just get himself killed. Azazel laughed sardonically. "As I said, your mother was the first hope I had in a long time. She was an angel, who chose to leave heaven. She wasn't cast out, and therefore, she was still permitted entrance. I wanted to use her. She was brought to me by descendants of my servants, but she refused to open the gates, even when I threatened her poor, demented sons, whom she had failed to tell about their powers."

He examined his nails, and I imagined prying each one off with a pair of pliers. "Unfortunately, that left me no choice but to destroy her and your father. I couldn't have either of them reporting back on anything they had heard. They died bravely, as did your grandfather."

Seth and I both lunged for him, but a brisk wind held us back, and as Azazel raised an eyebrow, I turned to see Sera, her hair blowing wildly around her face, her arms thrust towards us. Clapping, the dark angel quipped, "You are quite the controlling presence, I must say. It's too bad you sided with the heavens, my girl. I could have used the help keeping my witches in line through the years."

Hatred like I'd never seen before poured from Sera's eyes as she addressed Azazel. "Your impotence is not my problem." That statement didn't go over well.

I thought smoke was going to pour from the dark angel's nose. "I'll make this easy for you. Hand over the boy, and no harm will come to any of you."

"For how long?" I challenged. "I'm assuming your vengeance is going to be global and unforgiving. When you destroy heaven, and everything else with it, aren't we going down, too?"

"I wish to rule, not demolish," he countered, raising his voice. "And as the most high, I will grant you the highest privileges, just as I've promised my coven. After all, Jax McMullogh, it was through your efforts and those of Amelia Estelle that the key came into existence."

I seethed, and that fight I'd been holding out for was coming. I could sense my self-control cracking, and the tension in the air only built my determination to bash this asshole's head in. With Seth's help, I could take chunks out of the guy, and it was just what the doctor ordered. My blood boiled, my muscles bunched and strained, and I was filled with the adrenaline that would fuel me through a full-on war.

Seth was just as revved, and I could feel Sera's anxiousness in the shift in the air. We were ready to attack. "The boy has a name," I said in a deceptively calm voice. "His name is Blair, and he's my son. If you want him, you're going to have to plow through us to get him because I'll be damned if I'm handing him over to you."

"It's highly amusing that you believe you can protect the boy, just the three of you." He raised his arms, and a flash of lightning showed the alley filled with witches as far back as I could see. "You should have brought an army, boys, if you wanted a fair battle."

I had no idea how we were going to get through this. It was my worst nightmare, and as Amelia strode forward through the crowd to stand beside Azazel, her hair draped around her shoulders and her blue eyes piercing the night, I knew just how badly I wanted to serve her the justice she was due. I didn't care if Azazel had been the driving force; Amelia had chosen me and created my hell on earth.

"Darling, you don't stand a chance," she said in her sing-song southern drawl. She smiled sweetly, but I smelled vinegar in her tone. "Blair was meant for this purpose. All you're doing is delaying destiny. I have all the family in the world behind me," she gestured to the throngs of witches behind her, "and the power of a demigod at my side." She rested a hand on Azazel's shoulder. "Even the twelve year old boy can see it's best to join us. And it doesn't help your case that you lied about my death to him for so many years. How is he supposed to trust you?"

"You're a lying bitch," Blair spat, and I pushed him behind me as Amelia bared her teeth.

"You see? You're not even a fit parent, letting the little brat talk like that." She came at me, and I took up a defensive stance, knowing the conversation was over. It was time for action.

A blast of white light blinded me suddenly, and I realized how difficult it was going to be to fight hand to hand combat against magic. I swept a leg out blindly and connected with something, but I could only hope it was a body part. Seth was beside me, lashing out with fists, and I didn't know if he was landing shots or wasting his effort.

I saw Azazel throw a lightning bolt, lighting up the alley once again, and I seriously didn't understand how an entity that was supposedly banished beneath the earth and chained for all eternity could be standing before me and using this sort of power. It seemed very unfair.

I couldn't even concentrate on him as witches surrounded us, throwing those nasty multicolored balls of light I remembered from twelve years before with disgust. I dodged them the best I could, and as Amelia reared back to toss one my way, I could see clearly enough to duck and sweep my leg behind her heels, knocking her off her feet and sending the energy burst backward into the crowd of witches surging toward us.

Several of them wailed as the power burned them, and I was glad none of those giant fireworks had ever hit me or my son.

I launched myself on top of Amelia, who was in a bit of a panicked rage and reached to claw my face. I batted her hands away and, forgetting that I don't hit women, socked her square in the jaw. "You'll pay for that!" she shrilled. She rocked her legs up hard enough to throw me off her, but I rolled straight to my feet in fighting mode.

She took a moment to get up, just long enough for me to assess my surroundings and check on Blair. My son stood on the stoop at the door to the back of one of the shops on the main street, and he had grabbed what looked like a pipe from the ground. He swung it wildly, bashing at witches and blocking the fiery rainbow blasts. My chest swelled with pride, and it infused me with an even greater desire to fight.

Amelia threw another blast my way, and I

whirled out of the line of fire just in time to feel the searing heat as it passed too close to my shoulder and slammed into a witch who had apparently been about to drive a knife through my back. This was cutting it too close, and I turned a worried gaze toward Seth, who was knocking back five witches at a time. He kicked left, grabbed one with his right hand and tossed her over his shoulder to collide with another at his back, and he head-butted yet another.

The problem was, they kept getting up, and even with Seraphina creating a devastating wind of hurricane force that had them struggling to move forward, we weren't going to be able to clear them all. I had to concentrate on Amelia, and we had to find a way to send Azazel back to the miserable hell he'd crawled out of.

My ex-wife lunged at me, her face animalistic, drawn into a snarl with teeth bared, and I rounded a kick right into her ribcage. She lost her breath and her balance and fell to the side, gasping and holding her side. I took the opportunity while she was down to rush to Blair's side, too many of those damned witches gathering around him.

Sera stood in front of him, whipping wind at the army against us, but her face was drawn with the strain of using so much power, probably a difficult task in human form. As I slammed my shoulder through the witches surrounding my son, I saw Seth get sideswiped by a bright green blast, his arm instantly singed, and he growled in pain above the shrieking of the coven.

I knocked back at least ten of the bitches, who clawed at my legs through my jeans as they fell, shredding the material and drawing blood. But I clenched my teeth against the agony and shoved Blair behind me, knocking back every one of them in short order, no matter how many came my way.

Two voices sounded in my head, the first Amelia's, so high-pitched it made me cringe and nearly fall to my knees. But I pushed that away as the scent of cherry blossoms surrounded me, and I focused on Sera's voice.

Get Blair and Seth, and get around to the front of the store. Tell them Sera sent you. Hurry, I can't hold them long.

I didn't want to leave her, but I didn't have much choice. She was still holding her own, and as our eyes met for a brief moment, I prayed she would follow behind us before things got too desperate. I took one last look at the witches, their blasts slamming into each other and exploding over their heads, causing the bright fireballs to rain sparks on them, and I noticed Azazel, standing to the side, his eyes wide. His form wavered, and I could see through him now. He wasn't here, not in body. He was only a spirit, the mass of him still buried deep in the desert.

It gave me hope, and with renewed determination, I hollered to Seth, still in the midst of fighting, and he turned. I motioned for him to follow. I grabbed Blair in my arms and leapt from the stoop, landing behind Sera just as Seth powered his way out of the circle of witches who'd just charged him and joined us.

"Come on, we've got to get inside before…" But I didn't finish my statement. We were already running around the buildings, but I glanced back over my shoulder in time to see the culmination of our efforts fail in a way for which I would never forgive myself.

I love you, Jax. Sera's voice whispered through my mind, and I stared in horror as she released her wind, letting the throng of witches rush at her. "No!" I cried, turning back, but Seth grabbed my arm and yanked me along at full speed.

"Come on, damn it! We don't have time," he screamed. We rounded the corner, my mind barely processing what had happened. Blair had tears running down his face as we slammed into the voodoo shop, and the woman behind the counter, whose eyes were a creepy, milky white like she had cataracts, said, "I know why you're here. I can sense what you are." She pointed to her right. "At the end of the hall, you'll find a trap door leading underground. You must get through it and shut it behind you before they can follow you."

CHAPTER TWENTY SIX

I merely followed, struck by shock and dismay at what I knew had to have happened outside, especially as I heard an army of rushed footfalls racing toward the front door. Blair took my hand and jerked me in the direction the strange woman still pointed, and I followed without thought, Seth bringing up the rear as he shoved me forward.

The hallway was dark, and so was the room we entered, but a light shone from beneath the trap door, blinking like a strobe light. Blair rushed forward and pulled the door open, and Seth gripped my shoulder hard until I looked him in the eye. "Get your ass in gear, bro. This is the home stretch. Don't make Sera's sacrifice meaningless."

The words cut through me like a knife, and I lowered myself through the opening, reaching up and telling Blair, "Just jump, I'll catch you."

He didn't hesitate, and I set him on his feet as Seth grabbed the rope on the bottom of the trap door and hopped down. It closed just as the heard racing in our direction reached the room, and I breathed a sigh of relief. I looked around, the flashing light throwing me off, but Blair suddenly started walking down the long, dark, dirt corridor as if something was calling to him.

I glanced at Seth, saw him shrug in a flash of light, and we followed my son. There was a curve in the tunnel, and as we rounded it, I lifted my arm over my brow to shade my eyes from the brilliance of a golden light. Seth winced and did the same, and I could see the damage to his arm clearly. It wasn't good at all, and he needed medical care or it would scar badly, get infected easily, and perhaps even poison his blood. I had no idea what was in those magic fire blasts.

As my eyes adjusted slightly, I squinted and saw two giant golden doors, a single handle on the right one. They were inlaid with filigree so detailed I couldn't even begin to decipher the pattern in the blinding light. I stepped in front of Blair, who just stood staring at them, wide-eyed, without blinking, and I reached for the handle. It wouldn't budge.

"Step aside, weakling," Seth muttered, and he put some muscle into it.

I rolled my eyes. "Like you've ever been stronger than me."

"Dad, Uncle Seth, step back." Blair's voice was quietly reverent, and we both turned to gaze at him. He looked back and forth between us with a solemn expression. "Those are the gates. I'm the only one who can open them."

I felt stupid for even trying, and yet, I didn't want my son to be the one to do it. I felt like it was asking far too much for a twelve-year-old boy to save the world and thwart an angel as dangerous and evil as the devil himself. I gave Seth an inquisitive look, and he gave his typical shrug, stepping back and holding his arm.

I, too, moved out of the way, and Blair stepped forward, resting his hand on the knob for a second before twisting it and pushing the enormous door that should have weighed a ton open as if it was light as a feather. He walked in first, and Seth and I were both hesitant as we followed. A smiling figure clad in gold armor stood before us, just a bit taller than would have been natural for a human. He was ethereal, his hair a white blond over a pale face with eyes such a light blue they were almost transparent. He held a staff, a spear at the end of it, and somehow I knew who he was.

"Raphael," I gulped on a whisper.

He gave a short nod and knelt in front of us, addressing Blair directly. "Hello, young man. Tell me why you've graced us with your presence."

Blair glanced at me over his shoulder, and I nodded for him to go ahead. He bowed his head and took a deep breath before meeting those strange angelic eyes again. "My mother is the witch, Amelia Estelle, who has been helping an angel you cast down from heaven, Azazel. Together, they planned my birth, using my father. When he found out about their plan, he stole me and hid me so they couldn't hurt me, or anyone else. But they've been chasing me. Azazel wanted to use me to get into heaven for revenge."

I watched the angel's face, his anger that Azazel could have escaped his prison. I interjected, "Somehow, the coven managed to give Azazel the power to manifest himself as a spirit. He's still trapped physically, but he's been freed to wreak havoc in spirit."

Raphael nodded to me before turning back to Blair. "I'm assuming you were pointed to the portal by some other entity and followed by the coven."

My son nodded, and I could tell he was nervous, tired, angry and devastated, though he stood strong as he lifted his chin and told Raphael, "Seraphina, the air elemental sworn to protect the heavens, found us and led us here. She said I could only open the door once, so we planned to open and close it so everyone would stop chasing me. I just wanted to live a normal life. I didn't want anyone to get hurt."

His bottom lip trembled, and I went to him. I hadn't seen my son cry in years, and my broken heart shattered at the pain in his eyes. I hugged him close to me, and we both let a few tears fall for Sera. I didn't care what anyone in this room thought about a grown man crying; I'd vowed not to let anyone suffer, and I'd failed to protect my family as I'd wanted.

Seth cleared his throat, but when he spoke, his voice was still raspy. "They're out there now, banging at the damn door, and Seraphina…" He trailed off, and then whispered, "She gave herself to save us, and to keep them from getting to you."

"She has been a faithful servant for a very long time." Raphael's tone was deep, resonant, and troubled. "My child," he addressed Blair again, one strong, callused hand reaching out to touch my son's cheek, "you have been very brave, and I'm proud of your efforts. Because you have taken such burden upon your shoulders, you have managed to thwart a war in heaven that would lead to terrible things for those in the earthly realm, as well as chaos here. For that, you will be rewarded."

He stood, and I watched in silent awe as he strode toward the doors. With a wave of his hands, they swung open, and the golden light filled the hallway. As if projected on a giant movie screen, we watched the images flashing around us of Raphael stepping through the portal to face the gaggle of witches, hundreds of them running out of the shop and gathering in the street, under a dome of golden light that seemed to trap them.

Raising his arms over his head, Raphael

addressed them. "Women of the covens, hear me now. For your sins, you will reap your just punishment. I hereby sentence you to a mortal lifespan, spent on earth. Your powers are stripped, and none of you will be able to breed another child."

The wails were horrific, and I released my hold on Blair as we all covered our ears. Raphael held out his staff, and the rainbow colors of the fire they wielded shot to the tip of the spear in the most colorful rainbow I'd ever seen, broken and jagged like a million lightning bolts coming together. Several of the witches, older and spent beyond a mortal life, dropped dead and shriveled to little more than bones with skin pulled tight and gray over them.

"Jesus Christ, how old are those bitches?" Seth muttered.

I didn't even want to try to assess that, especially since Raphael was moving on. He seemed to simply float through the air, and suddenly, he was in darkness, his own glow providing the only visibility in the pit and revealing the tormented, twisted body of Azazel where he lay chained. "Awaken, betrayer."

Azazel moaned and opened his eyes, his body wrenching in agony as he wailed. "Silence!" The one word echoed a thousand times in the chasm, and Azazel made no further noise. "You have been given far too much opportunity to reform your ways, been allowed to remain in this realm too long. Even chained and trapped, you've managed to hurt and kill and seduce, and now, a reign you should never have had is ending. Azazel, Betrayer of the Lord and Heavens, liar to men, seducer of women, and power hungry beast, I now condemn you to the fires of hell, never to escape. May the demons have mercy on your eternal soul."

The ground beneath Azazel cracked and gaped, and my jaw dropped as I saw what looked like hot lava, with skeletal, burning souls reaching up to grab the dark angel and pull him into their midst. I covered Blair's eyes and turned away, the gruesome image far too much after what we'd been through in the last few days. My stomach couldn't handle it, and I didn't want it burned into my son's memory.

And then the angel stood before us again, his staff set aside and something else in his hand. It shone brilliantly, and as he knelt in front of Blair once again, I stared at it in complete disbelief. Seth moved toward us, his jaw slack, and ogled the short sword forged of what looked like solid silver.

"For your efforts, young master and sacred key, I bestow upon you a guardianship over the earth. As will your father and your uncle, you will be blessed with extraordinarily long life and will discover many threats to our existence. This angel sword contains the powers of the entire coven of witches that were destroyed tonight and will provide you with a warning when danger is near. It will also serve true and straight when you or any innocent soul needs protection most. It is a hefty responsibility, but you have passed a test this night that shall never be repeated. You have shown your true colors, and let it be known that you are a power unto yourself."

He held the blade out to Blair, and I watched with the satisfaction and emotion of a proud father whose son had done more than his share of good deeds in this lifetime. His mismatched eyes were wide and filled with excitement at this gift, and I could almost feel the power vibrating through the weapon as it swung close to me.

"The blade also gives you one other power," Raphael added with the first hint of a smile I'd seen on his face. "The spirits who have not found their way from one realm to the next sometimes need guidance, and they have always been drawn to you for your compassion and understanding. With this blade, you can offer them the final peace by protecting them and guiding them to the other side, for their next life."

A peaceful expression washed over my son's face, and I thought back to the first time I'd discovered him talking to a ghost. *She says only I can help her, but I don't know how.* Raphael had just given him the solution he'd been waiting for, and I knew that, above all else, Blair would want to trek back to that old house and rescue the sad girl.

I felt a knot forming in my throat just then, wondering if elementals had a spirit form. I would have loved the opportunity to say goodbye to Sera, to tell her that I loved her, too. I hated myself for being slow to admit my feelings for her, and now that it was too late, I raged inside, wishing I could just cross over long enough to kiss her, hold her one last time.

Blair nodded and whispered a nearly inaudible thanks, and Seth put a hand on his shoulder. My brother's eyes were puffy and red, and I realized he, too, felt the ache of Sera's death. She was supposed to be immortal, and I found that ironic and unfair. She'd retained her human form for our benefit. She could have flown away at any time, but she chose to stay and fight, to save Blair and the rest of us. It was the ultimate sacrifice, and I only wished now that I could take her place. My son had always had a father, but he'd never had a mother. I thought it would be a fair trade at this point.

I started to make my plea, but from a cloudy white doorway I hadn't seen before emerged another angel, this one smaller and more humble-looking than Raphael. I couldn't tell if the angel was male or female, its features androgynous, and it wore a white robe cinched at the waist with a rope woven from gold threads, an outfit that could have clad either sex. I didn't focus on that for too long though, as Sera's body suddenly materialized in his arms.

CHAPTER TWENTY SEVEN

I couldn't help myself; I dropped to my knees at the sight of her, broken and limp, and I couldn't make myself reach out or call to Blair as he rushed forward, forcing the angel to stop moving as he stood in front and brushed his small hand over her hair. She didn't flinch, didn't awaken, and she only looked like she slept peacefully. I didn't understand, couldn't comprehend why she didn't just wake up to his touch. She couldn't really be dead, could she?

Seth put a heavy hand on my shoulder, as if he couldn't hold himself up as he gazed at her. "I think I got a little more attached than I intended," he rasped. "It's too bad, you know. I was hoping I wouldn't have to worry about you having terrible taste in women anymore. She was a good one."

I felt like my lungs were going to burst as I held back the sobs. I knew in that moment I was going to offer myself in exchange for her life. Blair would be fine without me, and I certainly didn't have any desire for anyone else. I only wanted Sera, and if I couldn't have her, I could at least bring her back.

I pushed to my feet heavily and took a step toward the angel, Sera, and Blair, but Raphael's voice stopped me. "My new friends, please take a moment to grieve your friend, but also pay attention to Hamied, who has a gift for all of you to help soothe the sorrow of your loss."

I wanted to argue that nothing would relieve the pain in my chest, in the depths of my soul, at Sera's death, but I thought it was likely a very bad idea to make waves with the angel of vengeance. Instead, I stayed where I was, my gaze on Sera's beautiful face, wishing I could see those gold and silver eyes again, while Hamied addressed us.

"I wish I could take back the dreadful occurrences tonight that will be forever etched into your memories, my friends. But alas, even I can only work so many miracles. What I can do is give you a reminder of how beautiful the world really is. You see, energy never dies, it merely redistributes, and at this moment, each of you carries a small piece of your dear friend who was taken from you tonight." I squeezed my hands into fists, and I saw Blair hug himself, as if trying to feel that bit of energy within him.

"Tonight, you have lost all hope," the angel continued, and his tone grew more and more soothing, until I was lulled into a kind of calmness that I knew didn't come from within. "Things in life have suddenly become too much to handle. But I remind you that the world is still a beautiful place, and you should rejoice in the things you can still see and do."

"Yeah, well, just so you know, Ham, it doesn't

really feel so glorious right now. Aren't we entitled to wallow in our grief for a bit? We've barely caught our breath yet," Seth said, irritated and sounding exhausted.

"Yes, that is why I have come. You see, sometimes, we all need to see signs of the wonder that occurs around us in order to remain steadfast in our strength. Rest assured, I have come to offer a gift, and a sign that I pray will restore your faith in the magic of life and all the energy we possess inside us."

With those words, I felt a strange tug, as if someone had tied a rope to my chest and pulled. From the looks on Seth's and Blair's faces, they'd felt it, too. I narrowed my eyes and stared at Hamied, who placed a hand on Sera's chest. And miraculously, she gasped a deep breath.

Again, I was on my knees, this time overcome with disbelief and joy. Sera's eyes blinked open, and Hamied knelt to place her body in our arms, the three of us lined up on the floor and ready to greet the newly restored elemental.

Hamied spoke again. "Raphael summoned me, told me of your plight and your sacrifices, and I could not bear the loss you suffered. As an angel of miracles, I grant you this one. Your Seraphina is returned to you, whole and unharmed. May you all be happy together."

The angel placed a hand on Sera's shoulder as she sat up, trying to get her bearings. "And you, a faithful servant of the heavens, made the ultimate sacrifice for the greater good and gave up your immortal life. But more than that, you did it out of love for this family. For this reason, you deserve to have your miracle granted as well. From this moment forward, you are relieved of your obligation to protect the heavens and will only be charged with caring for your family, all of you protecting each other. And you will lead a human life on earth, as you wish, living a happy and long but mortal life with those you hold dearest."

I shook my head. "No, don't take that away from her. She doesn't deserve to come to an end. I…"

Sera held her fingers up to my lips to hush

me. "When one has existed as long as I have, immortality grows tiring. I have so enjoyed living as a human, cooking and sleeping and just being with you and Blair and even Seth." She gave him a rueful smile, and he winked back. "If you don't want me to stay with you, I understand, but I would choose to spend a long, mortal life with you. Loving you."

I couldn't believe what I was hearing. After all of this mess, which had actually been handled and the insurgents smashed, here we were again. I'd lost her. I'd lost Sera and been prepared to leave behind my life to give hers back to her. Now, I didn't have to make that choice because she was back with us, and yet, she thought I might not want her with me.

I stroked her cheek with the backs of my knuckles. "Sera, I would have given my life to bring you back. Blair needs you more than he needs me now. He needs someone he can look to as a mother. I would never want you to be apart from him." I hesitated, and I saw the pain in her eyes, so I smiled a crooked grin. "You didn't think that was all, did you?"

Her brows knit in confusion, and I pressed my lips to hers, ever so gently. "I'm in love with you, Sera. I can't imagine a future without you, and if we had really lost you for good, I would have been miserable."

Her golden eyes swirled, and the silver specks sparkled like glitter as she swallowed audibly. "Are you, Jax? Are you really in love with me?"

"Don't make me say it again, beautiful," I warned. I pulled her tight into my embrace, and I reached for Blair, drawing him in. I didn't have to reach for Seth, who stood over me and leaned down to envelope us all in the circle of his arms. "I love you, Sera, and you are as important to this family as anyone can be. You came to us and helped us and, somewhere along the way, you became one of us. And I became a fool for you in the process. I should have told you sooner, but I was in denial."

She pulled back and gazed into my eyes, shaking her head. "It doesn't matter. Now is the right time. Now is perfect." She pressed her palms to my cheeks. "I love you, too, Jax. I want to be mortal and spend every moment with you." She turned and bestowed the most adoring of smiles on my son. "And you, too, little man. You'll have to tell me everything. I missed so much of the action."

I winced at the reminder of seeing her die. But that was over now, and all I wanted was to go home and sleep for days, in the comfort of my home with my family. I gazed up at Hamied, whose face was so white I could barely make out features now, only the eyes. But I got the feeling a smile hid behind that light. "Thank you, my friend. Thank you so much." The angel nodded, and I turned toward Raphael, who stood sentinel like the soldier he was, watching us without a show of emotion.

"And thank you, for seeing justice done." I had an image of Amelia, sitting in the street, staring at lines in her hands that hadn't been there before and feeling tired and lost. And she was sobbing as she tried to manifest powers that didn't exist, alternately pressing her hands to her belly and sobbing. The corner of Raphael's mouth twitched, and I caught the desire to smile on his face. He felt good about his work tonight, too, and I couldn't blame him.

"Hey, boss, do you think you could work one more miracle for us?" I heard Seth ask, and I turned to find him grinning at Hamied.

The angel gave a short bow. "I shall certainly hear requests and make judgment calls."

So, the angel had a sense of humor. That was rich. Seth asked, "I'd rather not walk through the witchy bones and grossness outside to get back to the car. Do you think, maybe, you could find some way to beam us up or whatever, so the four of us and the Jeep and all the things land back at the house in Nevada until we figure out where to go from there?"

Hamied put on a show of thinking it over. "It's a tall order, but I believe all your travel and righteous battle qualify you for a bit of a reprieve. Take care, and perhaps we shall see you again one day."

And like that, we sat in the floor of the living room in the house in Nevada, Sera in my lap and Blair kneeling in front of us. Seth stood behind me, chuckling, and he took off to the front door, looking outside to see the Jeep parked in the driveway. He cackled even louder as he took note of all the luggage piled neatly in the hallway beside the dining room.

"Dude, I'm just saying, it's pretty damn sweet to have friends in high places, pun intended."

"That is the worst joke I think you've ever made, Uncle Seth," Blair told him. "And that's saying something because your jokes are typically pretty rotten."

"Hey, calm down over there. Just because you're the new prince of everything doesn't mean you can let you ego grow so big it won't fit through the fucking doorway." I laughed at Seth's joke and tussled my son's hair as my brother turned his attention to the woman in my arms. "And you, missy, don't go all Lazarus on me again, alright? I don't think my blood pressure can handle it."

Sera smiled at him. "And you don't spontaneously combust. I can't just blow on it and make it feel better anymore." As if to prove her point, she waved her hand in the air, and nothing happened.

I hugged her closer, inhaling deeply and told her, "It doesn't matter. That scent of cherry blossom is still on you, and as long as you're close enough, I'm happy."

"Get a room already," Blair moaned, but as I turned to scold him, he bore an enormous grin. He was happy to see me happy, and I couldn't have been more ecstatic. Maybe things hadn't gone quite the way I wanted. Amelia still existed, though I wondered for how long. I doubted she could live with herself as a powerless mortal. And there had been injuries and even death for our team. It was a devastating, terrifying night.

But in the end, we were here, and we were going to spend a lot of time figuring out where we wanted to settle down, no more limits and yet another person in our party to please. I wondered if Seth would go off on his own now, find his own way in life, but I didn't really want an answer to that yet. I wanted to start fresh and build a life, with all of us together, at least until we adapted to our new freedom.

THE END

ABOUT THE AUTHOR

Debut author, Natasha Dawn, was born in the border town of Lloydminster, Sask. before spending her early years in Moose Jaw, Sask. Her family later moved to Alberta for the booming oil industry. She's an avid reader of all things Paranormal and Romance so combining those two genres in her writing only comes natural. She dabbles in freelance writing while maintaining her full time career in Finance and being a mother of three children with her Husband in Lamont, AB.

Connect with Natasha online!
Twitter @AuthorNatashaD
Facebook
Goodreads

Want more from Natasha Dawn? Check out all of her available titles, and other great authors, through **www.guardianpublishing.ca** today!

The Sacred Key

Made in the USA
Charleston, SC
13 November 2015